DAVENPORT HOUSE 3

DAVENPORT HOUSE 3

A MOTHER'S LOVE

MARIE SILK

ISBN: 978-09973352-6-2 (print)
ISBN: 978-09973352-7-9 (ebook)

Marie Silk Publishing
P.O. Box 873
Hayden ID 83835

mariesilkpublishing@gmail.com

DAVENPORT HOUSE BOOKS BY MARIE SILK

For my children.

CHAPTER 1

Montgomery Manor House, Pennsylvania, circa 1892

"Louisa, please hold my hand," begged Maryanne Montgomery as she walked with her sister through the hallways of the manor house.

"What is it?" asked Louisa worriedly.

"I must tell Father something today, and I am afraid that he will never let me see you again," answered Maryanne in a scared whisper.

"What have you done? Is this why Father has asked to see us now?"

"No, he does not know yet. But I saw Sir George's carriage here earlier…"

"Your fiancé is here, then," said Louisa sadly.

"I cannot marry him, Louisa. It is impossible."

"Father will force you to marry Sir George, if he must," Louisa replied. "Won't you tell me what you have done?"

"I will tell you, but please do not be harsh with me. I—I have married John in secret," she stammered.

Louisa gasped. "Maryanne, you cannot tell Father such a thing! Your refusal to marry Sir George will be bad enough!"

"I know, but I am afraid that he will discover it some other way. Pray for me, that I might live through this day!" Maryanne squeezed her sister's hand as they walked into the grand drawing room where Mr. Montgomery and Sir George were waiting.

"Ah, my lovely daughters are here," greeted Mr. Montgomery as Maryanne and Louisa sat down on the sofa.

"I will leave you to it, Mr. Montgomery," Sir George said stoically. He stood up, nodded at Maryanne, then left the room.

"I have good news for you, Maryanne," her father said proudly. "Sir George has set a date for your wedding. He will be here next in August, and you will marry then."

Maryanne and her sister looked at each other. "Father, there is something I must say to you," Maryanne began timidly. "I cannot marry Sir George."

"You have been promised to him and you will marry him," declared Mr. Montgomery, unaffected by his daughter's words. "You may take your sister shopping with you for wedding clothes."

"But Father, I never wanted to marry Sir George. I have never even spoken with him before," Maryanne said anxiously.

"There will be time for that later," replied her father.

Maryanne tried again. "It is impossible for me to marry him."

"Why do you insist on contradicting me? Sir George will give you a proper home in London," he argued, becoming more agitated as the conversation went on.

"It is impossible, Sir," she cried with tears in her eyes.

"You will do as you are told!" her father bellowed angrily. The girls were silent as the sound of their father's voice echoed off the walls. The girls knew that when their father got this way, the wisest reaction was to say nothing at all.

Maryanne looked down at the floor and nervously broke the silence. "I am—already married."

"You are what?" he asked angrily. "It cannot be!"

"It is true. I have married John Smith," she confessed, shrinking back in fear.

Mr. Montgomery's eyes grew wide and his face was hot with anger. "My daughter—married to a gardener!" he cried. "I refuse to have my family ruined this way! I will order an annulment at once so this marriage you speak of will be nonexistent. You never had my permission to marry any other than Sir George!"

"An annulment is not possible, for I am already with child," she explained to her father, tears now flowing down her face. Louisa looked on in helpless anguish.

Mr. Montgomery huffed loudly from his red face. He suddenly picked up a vase from an end table and threw it violently toward Maryanne. The girls leapt from their seats when the vase came hurling across the room. It shattered to pieces against the marble fireplace. The sisters cowered behind the sofa while Mr. Montgomery glared at Maryanne. "You foolish ungrateful girl! Leave my presence and never attempt to come here again! You and your disgraced child will have nothing from me!"

Maryanne ran from the room in fear. Louisa was about to follow her, but her father grabbed her by the arm. "Do not dare go after that wretch. I forbid you to speak her name in this house again. I will ride after Sir George and persuade him to marry you. Make yourself presentable for when he returns with me." Mr. Montgomery let go of her arm and stormed out of the house.

Louisa whimpered as she ran to her sister's bedroom. Maryanne had a traveling case already packed and was struggling to move the hope chest from the foot of the bed. "Father has gone," Louisa told her breathlessly. "He is riding after Sir George to bring him back!"

Maryanne gasped. "They are going to kill John, I just know it! Help me, Louisa! Order the carriage at once!" Maryanne quickly left for the estate gardens behind the house. "John!" she cried frantically, running down the path through the hedges.

John Smith finally heard Maryanne's cries and ran to meet her. "What is it? Have you told him?"

"Yes, and I am afraid that he will kill you for it! We must leave now!" Maryanne and John hurried to the front of the house where a driver was waiting for them in the carriage.

Louisa stood anxiously near the carriage as her sister approached. "Go, quickly," she pleaded, handing Maryanne her purse.

"Thank you, Sister," replied Maryanne tearfully. She kissed Louisa on the cheek and climbed into the carriage with John. Maryanne was relieved to see that her hope chest along with her traveling case had already been placed in the carriage.

Louisa waved goodbye as Maryanne and John rode away. Tears ran down her face at the thought that she may never see her sister again.

"Has he hurt you?" asked John worriedly, gently placing his hand over Maryanne's belly.

"I was afraid that he was going to. He ordered me out of the house and to never come back," she answered sadly. "Perhaps I should be glad that I never need to see him again."

"Put him out of your mind. I will take care of you and the baby now," promised John. He turned to the driver and instructed that they should go to Philadelphia. John had rented a small room there after the night of their elopement.

When they arrived in Philadelphia, John took Maryanne's things inside while Maryanne lit a lantern to light the dark room. There was only a bed, small kitchen, and tea table and chairs. "Look, John," said Maryanne as she opened the purse that Louisa had given her. "My sister has given us twenty dollars. We will be able to buy food while we look for work."

John smiled at her and softly placed his hand over her belly, as he often did when they were alone. "You should not be working in your condition. Leave it to me. Our life may never be as grand as you are used to, but I will do my best to get us into a proper house." He pulled her close and kissed her gently. "I have waited so long for this day. I will spend the rest of my life seeing to it that you do not regret choosing me over Sir George."

Maryanne giggled as she sat on the bed. "I could never regret it. Although I do worry that I have left Louisa all alone with Father in that big house. She is only fifteen, poor dear. She helped our getaway tremendously by thinking to have the servants take my belongings to the carriage before we left. I knew that it would be like this when I told Father, but I was still afraid that I would lose everything from my other life, and the wedding dress that Mother had made for me. I want to give it our daughter when she is grown."

"Do you think we are having a daughter?" John asked with a smile.

"I am sure of it," she smiled back at him. "I have had dreams of having a girl and calling her Anna."

"Is it a family name?" asked John.

"It is not a family name, but it is what I call her in the dreams," Maryanne sighed. "This is the first time that I have felt safe in a long while. Thank you for bringing me here. I feel as though I can truly begin to live my life with you."

The months went by and John could not find the work that he had anticipated. They lived in a community with hundreds of others who had recently come to America and were also looking for work. For every one job were at least fifty eager men competing for it. John walked through the door of the small apartment after a long day of looking for jobs. Maryanne was inside sorting through her things.

"Perhaps I may sell some of my dresses," suggested Maryanne, looking at her large belly. "It is not as though I may fit into them now."

"It has not come to that yet," John replied, greeting her with a kiss. "I have good news. I was hired for work today."

"You were?" cried Maryanne excitedly. "What sort of work?"

"Deliveries. The pay is fifty cents for each delivery, so I need only make so many per night and we will be just fine," John smiled proudly.

"Fifty cents!" Maryanne cried with joy.

"We will eat like royalty tomorrow. You stay here and rest and I will be back in the morning with some chocolates for you," he said, winking at her.

"Oh, chocolate would be divine! But why must you make the deliveries at night?" Maryanne asked curiously.

"It is what the boss told me. I did not want to start asking questions and lose the chance of working for him."

Maryanne nodded. "Do be careful, John. The city is a different place at night."

"I will," he said, kissing her goodbye.

Maryanne was soon asleep on the bed, dreaming of the delectable breakfast they would share in the morning. She waited the next day for John to come home. He did not come in the morning as he had promised. Maryanne waited for him and fell asleep again in the afternoon. She was worried when it became dark and she still had not seen her husband. She wondered if he had come home while she slept, but left again so he did not wake her. Maryanne put on her cloak and visited the family in the connecting apartment. John was often next door, helping the family who came from Germany to learn English words. Maryanne knocked on the door and smiled when a young boy answered. "Good evening, Dear. Is my husband inside?"

The boy shook his head. "We've not seen him today, Ma'am."

"Your parents must be proud of how far you have come in your English. I know I am proud of you, Wilhelm. Would you please tell me if you see John tonight? He has a new job and I do not know when he will return."

"Yes, Ma'am," Wilhelm nodded. "Don't worry. I will take care of you until he returns."

Maryanne smiled and reached out to stroke his cheek. "I will see you tomorrow, Dear."

John did not return that night, or the next several days. Maryanne was soon out of money and had nothing to eat.

Marie Silk

She cried every day that John did not come home. She worried that he had died. She went to the hospital to look for him every night. She was so close to her delivery time that the nurses presumed Maryanne was there to have her baby. After looking for John at the hospital and speaking with the nurses again, Maryanne returned to the apartment in tears. She took a necklace from her hope chest and used it to pay a coachman to drive to her father's manor house.

The housekeeper at Montgomery Estate went pale when she saw Maryanne at the front door. "Miss Maryanne, I am not permitted to let you in," she whispered in a distressed voice.

"If you cannot let me in, then please send Louisa to come out and meet me. My husband is missing and I am in a desperate state!"

The housekeeper nodded with sad eyes and closed the door. Maryanne waited for what felt like hours for Louisa to finally emerge through the door.

"Maryanne!" she cried. Louisa tearfully embraced her sister. "You cannot be here! Father is home, and he will be furious!"

"John has been missing for days, and I know he must be dead. What am I to do, Louisa?" she pleaded.

"Oh, Sister! John is alive, but I am afraid he has been arrested," Louisa told her solemnly. "They say he may be in prison for life."

Maryanne gasped. "What happened?"

"I do not know, but when Father found out that your husband was arrested—"

"Who is at the door?" demanded an angry voice from behind her. Mr. Montgomery grabbed Louisa by the arm

8

and forcefully pulled her inside, slamming the door in Maryanne's face. Maryanne could hear his shouting on the other side of the door and she felt terrible for getting her sister into trouble.

"Father, I beg of you! She is due to have the baby at any moment," Louisa cried.

"They can both die in the streets where they belong! Get back to your room!" Mr. Montgomery raged.

Maryanne hurried away from the manor house and returned to the carriage that she arrived in. "Where to now, Miss?" asked the coachman.

"Take me to the hospital in Philadelphia," she replied frantically. "As quickly as you can."

A year had passed when John Smith received the news that a lady had come to pay his fines and arrange for his release. He was both elated and terrified to see Maryanne again. He never stopped thinking about his wife and baby. Now that he heard he was being released, he thought that Maryanne must be within the good graces of her father. He took a deep breath and left the prison gate. Outside of the prison, near the Montgomery carriage, stood Louisa.

"Louisa?" John reacted in surprise. "Where is Maryanne? And the baby?"

Louisa looked sorrowfully at John. "It has been a year since I last saw my sister. Father would not let her into the house when she came to us for help. I have been been trying all this while to see you released from prison. It is impossible with Father at home."

"If Maryanne is not with you, then where is she?" asked John worriedly.

"She has taken employment in a family home called

Davenport House in York County. I received a letter from her explaining all, but Father burned it soon after it arrived. You must go to her," Louisa urged while handing him several dollars.

John swallowed the lump in his throat and humbly took the money. "Does she want to see me?"

"She needs to see you. I would go to her myself if I could, but if Father found out…"

"I imagine you have risked an awful lot by coming to help me today," said John, watching the tears fall from her eyes. "How could I ever repay you?"

"You can repay me by taking care of my sister," she replied. "I must leave now so I can be home before Father returns."

John nodded at her. "Thank you, Louisa," he said sincerely, reaching for her arm to help her into the carriage. She winced in pain and quickly pulled her arm away from him. John felt terrible for hurting her. He had forgotten the bruises that Maryanne had brought with her from her father's house, and John now realized that Louisa must have endured the same. "Come with me to Davenport House," he offered gently. "I don't know how yet, but I will provide for you and Maryanne. Please, do not go back to him. You deserve better."

"I am afraid I do not have a choice," she answered painfully. The carriage took Louisa away, and John went to Davenport House to find his wife.

Davenport House, York County, Pennsylvania, Summer of 1915

John Smith could feel the tears stinging behind his eyes while remembering those days of the past. When he found Maryanne after his release from prison, John did not know that he would only have seven years with his wife before influenza took her away. He had been forced to learn how to live without her in the years since. He knew that someday he would have to tell his son Ethan the truth about what happened before—he just did not know how.

CHAPTER 2

I t was a sunny afternoon in the magnificent gardens behind Davenport House. The Davenport sisters, Mary and Clara, were having a walk to admire the flowers while discussing Clara's wedding plans for the summer. Clara wore a delightful blue afternoon dress that day, while Mary wore the traditional black mourning dress that had been her attire since the death of her father. Mary was raised as a proper heiress in Davenport House, while Clara, who was the housekeeper's daughter, attended to Mary as a maid. It was recently revealed that Mary and Clara were both from the same father, who was the late Master of Davenport House. Mary inherited the mansion on the thousand acre estate and was happy to share the wealth her newly discovered sister.

"Have you decided on a dressmaker?" Mary asked Clara, who had recently become engaged to the neighbor. Wedding planning ruled the conversation of every day since.

"There is one lady I would like to hire," answered Clara.

"Mrs. Livingston has a shop in Philadelphia. I wanted to ask you if I may have the carriage tomorrow to see her."

"I am afraid that I will be using the carriage for Yorktown tomorrow. Can you go the next day?" asked Mary.

Clara was disappointed. "Her shop will be closed. I suppose I can wait until next week."

"I understand that you want to have your dress started as soon as possible," Mary said thoughtfully. "Take the carriage tomorrow and I will postpone my errands for another day."

"Are you certain, Mary? I do not want to spoil your plans," said Clara hesitantly.

"I will make other arrangements, don't worry," Mary assured her.

Mary went into the house to look for Mrs. Price, who was the estate overseer as well as Clara's mother. Abigail, Mary's companion, passed Mary in the Hall.

"Good afternoon, Mary," greeted Abigail. "Will you be riding today? I am about to see Ethan at the stable."

"I think I will ride later, but for now I am looking for Mrs. Price. You go on ahead without me," replied Mary.

Abigail smiled. "I will tell Ethan. I have finished making this set of riding clothes for myself so I will not need to borrow yours anymore. I am glad that we will go to to the cobbler's shop tomorrow. I'm afraid my boots are nearly worn through."

Mary cringed. "Oh dear. I had forgotten that you needed to go to Yorktown tomorrow as well. I told Clara that she could have the carriage to see her dressmaker in Philadelphia. I will explain to her," Mary said, feeling conflicted.

"It is alright, Mary. Clara should take the carriage," offered Abigail, trying to hide her disappointment. "My boots will hold up another day or two, I am sure. I understand that Clara is eager to get her dress started."

"Now I feel that I have let both of you down," Mary sighed. "I must find Mrs. Price to see if there is anything we may do about this."

She found Mrs. Price in the library reviewing the tenant accounts. "Good afternoon, Miss Mary," greeted Mrs. Price.

"Good afternoon. I would like to speak with you about purchasing an automobile sooner than we originally intended. With Clara and Abigail planning their weddings at the same time, and the things that I must do in town, one carriage will no longer do," explained Mary.

"I am afraid that two of our tenants are behind on their rents just now, but perhaps sometime next month," answered Mrs. Price.

"Are there no other options to consider? I was hoping for this week."

"I have thought of something, but was not sure how you would receive the idea. An automobile for the house would mean less use of the carriage. Perhaps we may sell the carriage horses. The price they would bring will make up the shortage in rents, and you could purchase your car sooner," suggested Mrs. Price.

"I suppose it would not be the end of the world if we had to part with the carriage horses," Mary thought aloud. Then she smiled. "Very well, Mrs. Price. Please see to the sale of the horses so that we may finally have our motor car.

It is time that we began living with the rest of America in the twentieth century."

Mary went to the stable to see Ethan, the young man who cared for the horses and stable of Davenport Estate. "Good afternoon, Miss Mary," he greeted in his usual quiet way.

"Good afternoon," Mary replied. "I have just been speaking with Mrs. Price about selling the carriage horses so we may purchase a motor car."

Ethan held his breath. "You will sell the horses?" he asked skeptically. He was anxious about the recent transition from horse to car that put many stables boys out of work.

"We are only parting with the carriage horses. We will keep the other three of course," answered Mary.

"For now…" Ethan muttered under his breath.

Mary giggled at his moody reaction. "Everything will be fine, Ethan. You will always have a home here. I promise."

"What about Peter Ross?" asked Ethan.

Mary cringed. "I suppose I had not considered what would happen to our carriage driver. Perhaps he may take driving lessons and become our new chauffeur."

Ethan shook his head. "He is old, Mary. His eyesight is going."

Mary became frustrated. "Do you have any better suggestions? It seems that I cannot make everyone happy with my decisions for the house."

"I am sorry," Ethan told her. "I know you are doing your best. Part of me is worried that I will be out of a job and then I could never provide a proper house for Abigail."

"How are your wedding plans coming along?" asked

Mary, grateful to change the subject. They could hear Abigail riding back to the stable just then.

Ethan was quiet. He did not know how to tell Mary that he had not spoken of wedding plans since his engagement to Abigail weeks ago. Ethan lived in the apartment above the stable with his father, who also worked on the estate as the groundskeeper. Ethan figured that Abigail would not want to live in his small apartment after she had been living in the mansion as a lady's companion. He smiled apologetically at Mary for not answering, then went to assist Abigail.

"Just a moment, Ethan," said Abigail when she saw Mary. "Have you come to ride, Mary? I will accompany you, if you wish."

"No, I have only come to talk with Ethan about some changes. He is unhappy with me," Mary teased.

Ethan helped Abigail down from her horse. "Miss Mary is going to sell the carriage horses," he told her mournfully.

Abigail took Ethan's hand and looked into his eyes. "I am certain that everything will be alright," she assured him. Ethan smiled back at her. One look from Abigail made him forget all of his worries. His heart was filled with love for her.

"I am returning to the house now, but I am not sure that I should leave you two without a chaperon," Mary giggled.

"I will go with you, Mary," replied Abigail as she slowly released Ethan's hand. She was glad to be marrying such a kind, handsome man, but Abigail wondered why he would not talk about the wedding at all.

Mary and Abigail walked back to the house, and Mary

thought she would try her question again. "How are your wedding plans coming along, Abigail?"

"I am unsure," Abigail answered shyly.

"What do you mean?"

"Ethan has not said anything about it. I am too embarrassed to mention the wedding myself," she answered.

"I do not understand. He spoke to me of how much he wanted to marry you. I wonder what he is waiting for."

"I wish that I knew. I already have my wedding dress, at least," answered Abigail.

"How wonderful! Did you make it yourself?" asked Mary. She knew that Abigail used to be a seamstress.

Abigail smiled to remember how she got the dress. "Ethan gave it to me. It belonged to his mother," she replied shyly.

Mary gasped. "Oh! It is lucky that Ethan was able to save it from the stable fire. May I see the dress? I did love Ethan's mother dearly. She was so kind to me. I would be grateful to see anything that belonged to her."

Abigail smiled. "Come to my room and I will show you. It is lovely."

Clara Davenport walked toward the farmhouse where her fiance lived with his two children. Phillip Valenti had come to America from Italy and recently moved to York County from Pittsburgh after his wife passed away. Phillip desired that his two young children would be raised on a quiet farm in the countryside. The Valentis' farmhouse was just a short walk from Davenport House.

"Miss Clara!" Phillip's four-year-old little girl greeted Clara at the door.

"Good afternoon, Gabriella," Clara said with a smile. "Is your papa in the house?"

"Papa is outside. I must stay in the house and keep Donnie out of mischief," Gabriella said about her three-year-old brother.

Clara giggled. "I will go find your papa. You keep watching your brother." She walked around to the back of the house and found Phillip by the fruit trees. Clara's blond hair shone brightly in the sun and her elegant dress brought out the blue in her eyes. Phillip smiled when he saw her.

"Good afternoon, Clara. You look beautiful. I must be the luckiest man in Pennsylvania," he said, reaching for her hand to kiss.

"Why, thank you. You look handsome yourself," Clara remarked, admiring his muscular build and attractive face. Phillip chuckled in response. He had been working on the garden all day and it showed. He was not sure if he should believe Clara, but he was happy to hear her say it anyway. Clara continued, "It is funny that Gabriella can take care of Donnie, when she is so young herself."

Phillip nodded. "She will be five in a few days. I remember my sisters being made to cook dinners by that age. I was hoping you could teach her, since I am no good at cooking myself."

Clara laughed. "I am no cook, but I will try. I am going to Philadelphia tomorrow to meet a dressmaker."

"Oh, then I will not see you tomorrow," remarked Phillip. "I hope you have a pleasant journey."

"I could be there and back in half the time with a motor car. I am going to ask my mother if I can buy one for myself. I get weary of always asking Mary if I may use the carriage. Anyway, we will need a car when we marry. I thought perhaps we could go to New York for our honeymoon," said Clara.

Phillip smiled. "Anything you wish, my dear."

"I have already met with the minister at Yorktown. You will like the church, I am sure. It is not very fancy but it is where we can be married," said Clara.

Phillip raised his eyebrows in surprise. "Oh? I suppose I have not seen the church yet."

"We should go together in the new car," Clara giggled. "I cannot wait."

Abigail and Mary stood in Abigail's room, admiring the flowing white wedding gown. "Oh, it is breathtaking! How lucky you are," said Mary. "Have you tried it on already?"

"Every night," Abigail confessed shyly. "It fits splendidly. I only hope that I may wear it for real before I grow old," she teased.

"Would you like for me to speak with Ethan about why he has not said anything about the wedding? He is rather shy, but I am happy to ask him for you," suggested Mary.

"It is generous of you to offer. I think I should speak to him myself, though. Perhaps he does not think that I will be happy living in the apartment with him," said Abigail.

"Well, would you? Be happy living so simply, I mean," asked Mary.

"Of course I would be. As long as we are together, it does not matter to me where we live. I had always lived a simple life until I became your companion. I am happy either way," she answered.

Mary smiled. "I will miss you living in the house with

me. I am glad that my best friends will be marrying each other, although I am rather envious if I am to be honest."

Abigail looked serious for a moment. "Mary, I have wanted to ask you, but I did not know how to say it. Does it cause you any pain that I have agreed to marry Ethan? I know you have been close to him since childhood."

Mary looked surprised, then giggled. "You are kind to worry for me. I have loved Ethan my whole life, but not in the way that you love each other. I only want him to be happy and looked after. I would rather no one in the world marry him but you. When I said I was envious, I did not mean about Ethan. I meant I wish it was me who was getting married. I suppose I am envious for this beautiful dress as well. I cannot wait to see your wedding."

"I am certain it is only a matter of time before William asks you. Do you know what he said to me in the gardens just weeks ago?" questioned Abigail.

Mary's heart began to beat faster. "What did he say to you?"

"He asked me when the days of your mourning tradition would be complete," Abigail replied with a smile.

Mary gasped. "So William *is* waiting for me to be out of mourning. It feels as though it has been ages since Father died. It is difficult to believe it has only been two months. I suppose it feels longer because so much has happened since then." Mary paused for a moment. "Did you know that William has kissed me?"

"What?" gasped Abigail. "When did this happen?"

Mary smiled but her cheeks were pink with embarrassment. "It has happened twice. The first time was at the clinic when he told me that he was leaving for Philadelphia. The other time was here at the house before he went back to the clinic. It was heavenly," Mary said, covering her face with a pillow from Abigail's bed.

Abigail giggled. "Well, now it is I who am envious. I have never been kissed. So you are ahead of me in that respect." The girls laughed together and continued to admire the beautiful wedding gown hanging from the wardrobe.

At the dining table that night sat Mary and Abigail, Clara and her mother Mrs. Price, and Ethan and his father John Smith, who Mary had invited to dine with the family every night. Mrs. Price's sister had worked as the cook at Davenport House after the former cook went missing. Catherine Price was well-known for her delicious meals, and everyone at the table felt fortunate to have her as the cook.

"We will be buying a motor car soon," announced Mary happily. Clara seemed to perk up at this news.

"A wonderful idea, Mary. I will be getting one for myself as well. We will have two cars here!" Clara said excitedly. Mrs. Price gave Clara a look, but did not say anything. Mrs. Price managed Clara's finances and was well aware that Clara could not afford a car anytime soon.

"I do feel badly for putting poor Peter Ross out of a job as our carriage driver. I suppose we will have to make inquiries for a chauffeur," Mary mentioned.

"Phillip can drive cars," said Ethan suddenly. "He has told me that he is looking for work to support his family."

"That won't be necessary, Ethan," Clara stated firmly. "Phillip is soon to be married to me. He should not need to demean himself to such a job as driving others around. Unless it is our own car, of course."

The room went quiet for a moment. No one knew how

to respond to Clara's statement. Mary finally broke the awkward silence. "Have you and Phillip set a date?" she asked.

"We have not decided on the date, but I am hoping for August when my dress should be done. I will ask Mrs. Livingston how long the dress will take to finish when I visit her tomorrow."

Abigail could not take her eyes off of Ethan. He looked exceptionally dashing tonight in his black suit and tie. Abigail sat across the dining table from him and wished she could lean over and kiss him right then. Ethan smiled at Abigail when he noticed her looking. Abigail became suddenly shy and looked down at her plate. "The gardens will be lovely in August, I am sure. Will you have your reception here at the house?" Abigail asked Clara, trying to participate in the conversation.

"I believe so," answered Clara. "I have already spoken to the minister of the church at Yorktown. It is not a grand building, but it will have to do for the ceremony."

"My boy was baptized from that church," mentioned John Smith. "The minister is a good man."

"Clara was baptized there as well," remarked Mrs. Price.

"I expect all of us were," said Mary. "Not Abigail, of course, since she only moved here recently from Johnstown."

Abigail smiled in response. Dinner was soon finished and most everyone retired to bed. Fiona, the young housekeeper of Davenport House, found Clara walking toward the grand staircase for her bedroom. "Mr. Valenti here to see you, Miss Clara," Fiona announced. "He waits for you outside the front door."

"He is here now?" asked Clara in bewilderment. "I hope the children are alright." She went out to meet him in front of the house. "Phillip, whatever is the matter?" she asked as she approached him in the dark.

"I am sorry to bother you like this, Clara. I came as soon as the children fell asleep. I just wanted to speak with you," he said anxiously.

"Oh, I see. Well, I am glad that you have come to visit. You will never believe what the others said about you at dinner tonight," said Clara.

"What did they say?" asked Phillip worriedly.

"Mary is wanting to hire a chauffeur for the new motor car she will buy. Ethan suggested that you could fill the position," Clara explained, shaking her head.

Phillip raised his eyebrows in surprise. "I would like that very much. The wages would be welcome."

"Oh, Phillip, you don't want to drive people around for a living. Besides, a Davenport lady cannot marry a chauffeur. I thought you would like to be a gentleman and we could live off my inheritance as other ladies and gentlemen do," explained Clara.

"I suppose we can speak about that later. There is something more urgent I must say to you tonight," said Phillip.

"What is it?" Clara questioned, suddenly panicking that Phillip may be having second thoughts.

"I—I don't know how to say this, but I must tell you plainly. I am Catholic, and I cannot get permission to marry you unless you agree to raise the children in the Catholic church," he said worriedly, wringing his hat in his hands.

Clara's eyes grew wide. She suddenly looked around to make sure that no one could hear them. "You are

Catholic?" she whispered frantically. "Why have you not said before now?"

"I am afraid it has become a habit stay silent about it. When you spoke of meeting the minister today, I realized I had to say something."

"I assumed everyone here was Protestant," said Clara. "Why do you need your church's permission anyway? You can convert and not worry about what they say."

Phillip looked down and sighed. "I am Italian, Clara. My family has been Catholic for generations. It is not as simple as converting. I would not ask you to convert for me. I only need to know that you will allow the children to be raised Catholic."

"How can I consent to such a thing? My mother would faint," Clara said.

"I should have said something sooner. I guess I was caught up in the feelings and did not think," said Phillip sadly.

"Yes, you should have said something sooner! I was just about to leave to Philadelphia to have my dress made!"

"Perhaps we may come to a solution—" began Phillip.

"I don't see how we can. There are some things that I can bend on, and I am afraid this is not one of them," Clara interrupted. "Unless you convert. It is the only way we can be married."

Phillip hung his head. "Perhaps we can speak of it later after you have had time to think about it."

Clara huffed angrily. "If you will not convert for me, then you must not have wanted to marry me so much in the first place!" She turned to go back into the house. Just after she opened the door, she turned her head to say to him, "Perhaps you should take the chauffeur job for Mary after all. Without my inheritance, you will certainly need the money." She closed the door forcefully and went to her bedroom to cry. She thought about how humiliated she would be to tell everyone that the wedding she had boasted about for weeks—was now off.

CHAPTER 3

The next morning at breakfast, Mary, Abigail, and Mrs. Price were at the dining table. "There is good news for you, Miss Mary," Mrs. Price began. "We have a buyer for the carriage horses. I have already informed Ethan, and he will ready the horses for the buyer next week."

"Wonderful, Mrs. Price. Have you informed Peter Ross of the change?" asked Mary.

"I have, Miss Mary. I offered him a months' wages while he looks for new work," she answered.

"I hope he does well. This is the difficult part about being owner of a house. I wish we never needed to let a servant go," Mary said.

"You are kind to even think of a servants' plight, Mary," Abigail mentioned. "I am not sure that many Mistresses would think much of sending a servant away."

"Please tell your fiance that he need not worry about being next," Mary said playfully. "I would die if I did not have my horses. Dolly means as much to me as any person. I could not bear to be without her."

"I am sure that Ethan will be glad to hear it. I plan to speak with him today," said Abigail, looking at Mary.

"I hope all goes well," Mary answered kindly.

"Post for you, Miss Mary," announced Fiona, presenting a letter on a silver tray.

"It is from William," Mary said excitedly. She opened the letter and began to read. "Oh dear. He writes that I should not come to the clinic due to an outbreak of fever." Mary frowned. "I hope William does not catch it. Now I will be worried for him even more than usual."

Abigail looked at Mary compassionately. "I am sorry for your disappointment, Mary. Perhaps it was a good thing that Clara needed the carriage today for the dressmaker. If you and I had gone to Yorktown as we planned, we may have missed William's letter warning us not to visit the clinic."

Mary sighed heavily. "Yes, I suppose it may have worked out for the better. William mentioned before that his telephone would be installed this week. I hope that he rings soon so that I may speak to him, since I cannot visit him in person. I think I will be in the library today to catch up on my reading. That way I will be near the telephone if William does ring."

After breakfast, Abigail went to the stable to visit Ethan. She was surprised to see the carriage horses grazing in the pasture. "I thought that Clara had already left to Philadelphia," she remarked confused.

"Peter Ross had the carriage ready for hours but Clara did not come out. We just let the horses in the pasture until she is ready to leave," answered Ethan. He went to get a saddle for Amethyst, the horse that Abigail preferred to ride above the others.

"Wait…Ethan…I did not come to ride. I want to speak with you," said Abigail timidly.

"What is it?" he asked in concern.

"I wonder if we should be planning what we will do for our wedding."

"Oh," said Ethan, looking down at the floor. "I am saving my wages so that I can buy a proper house for you. I do not know how long it will take."

Abigail took his hand and looked into his eyes. "I am grateful to you, Ethan. But does this mean that you do not want to be married until a house can be bought?"

He gently put his arms around her. "I want to marry you now," he whispered. "I did not want to ask a fine lady like you to live in a stable with me."

Abigail sighed in relief. "Is that all it is? I am happy to live with you, if your father is agreeable to my staying here."

"Are you certain, Abigail?" asked Ethan. "Why don't I show you the apartment again. My pa is up there now. You should take a good look before you decide."

They walked upstairs to the modest apartment. It was equipped with a small kitchen, small sitting room, bathroom, and two bedrooms. The ceilings were very low on the both sides where the A-framed roof slanted down. John Smith was asleep on one of the chairs in the sitting room. Ethan and Abigail tried to be quiet so they did not wake him. Ethan showed Abigail his bedroom from the doorway. There was a bed and a small chest of drawers. "Do you sleep on your bed or on the floor?" Abigail asked him with a giggle. She had found him sleeping on the floor once before in one of the most embarrassing moments of her life.

Ethan smiled and chuckled. "I do sleep on the floor. The bed is too soft for me. You might get the bed all to yourself."

"I hope not," Abigail said, then began to blush. "Sorry, I don't know why I said that." She covered her cheeks with her hands.

Ethan put his hands around her waist. He looked into her eyes intently, then looked toward her lips. Abigail held her breath in anticipation as he slowly leaned into her.

"Son?" interrupted the voice of John Smith. Both Ethan and Abigail jumped.

"I was just showing Abigail the apartment, Pa," Ethan explained sheepishly. Abigail knew that her face was now redder than ever, but she thought it might be worse to cover it with her hands now.

"Good afternoon, Young Lady," John Smith greeted.

"Good afternoon, Mr. Smith," she replied. Ethan and Abigail seated themselves on the chairs in the sitting room.

"It is not as grand as Davenport House," remarked John Smith. "But it suits us just fine."

"It is a lovely apartment, Mr. Smith. I have shared a home this size with my ten brothers and sisters, so any home feels spacious after that."

"You have ten brothers and sisters?" Ethan asked incredulously.

"I do. They live in Johnstown with my father. They are younger than I am," explained Abigail.

"I don't know what it is like to be crowded like that since I am an only child. I cannot imagine living with so many," replied Ethan. John Smith abruptly stood up from his seat and went out the door.

Abigail looked at Ethan in dismay. "I hope I have not upset him," she said worriedly.

"I do not see how you could have," replied Ethan.

"Perhaps he does not want me to live here. I should have waited for you to ask him before I said anything," suggested Abigail.

"I will talk to him, Abigail. I cannot imagine that is the reason. Pa is very fond of you. Do not worry," Ethan said, holding her hand in his. "Everything will be alright."

Mary was reading in the library when the room was suddenly filled with a loud ringing sound that startled her out of her chair. She picked herself off the floor while the ringing continued. She laughed when she realized what the sound was—the house's first telephone ring since it had been installed. Mary awkwardly took the receiver in her hand and held it to her ear, hoping that she was doing it correctly. Then she realized that she did not know what to say.

"Davenport—House," she stammered.

"Mary?" asked a familiar voice through the receiver.

"William! Good afternoon!" she greeted cheerfully. Her heart was racing at the sound of his voice.

"Good afternoon. Did you receive my message about avoiding the clinic?" William asked quickly.

"Yes, I received it just this morning. Are you alright?" asked Mary.

"I am alright. Is anyone at the house ill?"

"No, we are well," Mary answered. She could hear William sighing in relief.

"I am glad to hear it. There is an outbreak in town. It looks like typhoid, but I have yet to determine the source.

You should stay at the house until we get it contained, just in case."

"We will. Thank you for warning us," Mary answered.

"I look forward to seeing you again," William said quietly.

"I look forward to it as well," Mary replied.

"Goodbye, Mary"

"Goodbye, William." Mary placed the receiver back in its cradle and could feel her heart pounding in her chest. It was a thrilling sensation to hear the voice of the man she loved, even if she could not see him face to face. Mary's expression was set in a smile for a long while afterward.

Abigail returned to the house, still worried that Ethan's father did not want her to live in the apartment. She walked up the grand staircase and observed one of the housemaids on the landing. "Bridget," began Abigail. "Have you seen Clara today?"

"She is in her room, Miss Abigail," replied Bridget. "She asked for her meals to be sent there for the rest of the day."

"I see. Thank you, Bridget," Abigail said politely. Bridget left for the servants' stairs and Abigail stood awkwardly on the upstairs landing, wondering if she should check on Clara. Clara's room was on the opposite side of the house from the other family bedrooms. Abigail took a deep breath and went to the staircase on the right, then down the long hallway to Clara's bedroom. She knocked on the door.

"Come in," called Clara in a distressed voice.

Abigail walked in to find Clara still in bed wearing her nightclothes. "Clara, are you ill?" she asked in concern.

Clara shook her head. "I just don't want to see any-one," she scowled.

"Oh, I am sorry. I will go," Abigail apologized and turned for the door.

Clara began to cry loudly. "The wedding is off! I don't want to face the others to tell them," she spoke between sobs.

"Oh, Clara," Abigail said compassionately. She gave Clara a handkerchief, then sat on a chair close to the bed. "I am terribly sorry. Has something happened? You do not need to tell me if you do not wish to."

"Phillip came to the house last night to tell me that he is part of the Roman Catholic Church! Can you believe it?" Clara asked incredulously. When Abigail did not seem to react, Clara continued, "You do not look as surprised as I was."

"Um—well, his family comes from Italy," Abigail stammered.

"We cannot be married unless one of us converts," Clara went on. "If he really loved me, he would convert, but he refuses. Our wedding can never happen."

"I am sorry for your disappointment," Abigail said softly. "Is there anything that I can do?"

"Just tell the others so that I do not have to. I am frightened to see my mother's face when she finds out that I was engaged to a Catholic all this while."

"I will tell them," Abigail promised. She went out the door and could feel her heart sinking in her stomach. She felt badly for Phillip Valenti being rejected for the second time. It was not so long ago that Phillip had asked Abigail to marry him, but she declined because she was in love with Ethan. Her heart now ached for the young children who believed that they would have a new mother when Clara married into the family. Abigail wondered how

Phillip would tell the children. She was not sure how she would tell the others in the house.

John Smith was not at the dinner table that night. Abigail became increasingly worried that he must be upset with her. Ethan gave her hand a gentle squeeze under the table to reassure her that everything was alright. Mary excitedly described her first telephone call with William. The others were quiet throughout the meal.

"Mrs. Price, did Clara say if she would be staying overnight in Philadelphia?" asked Mary curiously.

"She did not tell me, Miss Mary," Mrs. Price answered.

"Um…Clara did not go to Philadelphia," Abigail stated nervously.

"What do you mean? Where has she been all day?" asked Mary. Mrs. Price also looked on in surprise.

Abigail cleared her throat. "Clara is in her room."

"She is not ill, is she?" asked Mary. "William has said that people are coming to the clinic with typhoid fever." Mrs. Price held her hand over her heart when Mary mentioned it.

"Clara is not ill," Abigail replied quickly to save Mrs. Price the worry. Abigail took a deep breath before she continued. "She has called off the wedding and does not wish to see anyone."

The room was quiet as Mrs. Price and Mary looked at Abigail in shock. "Did she say why?" Mary finally asked.

Abigail looked down at her plate. She was terribly uncomfortable having to relay this information, but she had promised Clara. "They had a dispute, and have decided not to marry," she explained quietly, hoping that she would not be asked any more questions. She felt Ethan squeeze her hand again and she did not know if it made her feel better or worse.

"Has the buyer asked anything more about the carriage horses before they decide, Mrs. Price?" Ethan asked, changing the subject.

"They seem certain of the sale. Only, they need a week before they will have the funds," she answered him. "We are still able to purchase the automobile for the house while we are waiting." Mrs. Price was distracted by the revelation about Clara's broken engagement. Much to Abigail's relief, no one said another word about Clara and Phillip Valenti at dinner that night.

Ethan had promised Abigail that he would talk to his father after dinner. He went to the apartment above the stable and seated himself across from where his father sat in silence. "Pa? Is everything alright?" he asked.

"I'm afraid not, Son," answered John Smith.

"Abigail is worried that you might not want her to live in the apartment with us. Is that what is bothering you?" Ethan questioned nervously.

"Abigail is a fine young lady. I've thought so since the first time I saw her. I would not mind one bit if she lived here, if it is what you and she want," he answered solemnly.

"She will be relieved to hear it, then. The thing is, you seemed upset when we spoke of the living arrangement earlier. Will you tell me what is wrong?" Ethan asked. His father was usually quiet and did not give much information. Ethan got used to him sometimes never answering at all.

"It was because of what you said about not having any

brothers or sisters," John Smith said quietly, feeling tears forming in his eyes. "Your ma always wanted a big family."

"Oh. I am sorry about that, Pa. I know you would have if it were possible," Ethan replied.

"You were not the only child," John Smith said with a shaky voice.

Ethan looked straight ahead at his father in stunned silence. When Ethan found his voice, he asked, "Do you mean that I have brothers and sisters that I don't know about?"

"You would, if not for my mistakes. I messed up bad, Son…before you were ever born. I lost my job and moved with your ma to Philadelphia. I got a job working for some men there. They were bad men, but I turned a blind eye to it because I needed the wages. I got arrested one night when your ma was near ready to deliver our first child. I left her with no money or food. It was all my fault." Tears were now falling down his anguished face. "When she told me she lost the baby after that, I knew it was because of me. I should have been there to help. I spent the rest of my time with your ma trying to make up for it. But how could I make up for the loss of a child?" He buried his face in his hands as Ethan looked on silently.

"I'm sorry, Pa. I don't know much about women and childbirth. But I've seen enough foals delivered to know that sometimes, there is nothing you can do. It is nobody's fault," Ethan said sadly.

"It was my fault. Your ma's death was, too. I failed bad. The doctor kept saying he was too busy with other sick folks, but I should have hog-tied him and brought him to the house that is what it took. Sometimes now, I don't even want to live anymore. When the old stable caught fire, I almost hoped it would take me with it. If you had not come to help me, I would have laid down right there in the fire and let the memories die with me. But I keep living for you. There is nothing else that keeps me going on this earth."

Ethan was holding back his own tears. He did not know if there was anything he could say that might alleviate his father's sorrow. "You did everything you could, I am sure."

John Smith sighed heavily. "Now I have told you everything, Son. There is something more I must show you." He kneeled to the floor in front of Maryanne's hope chest and lifted the heavy wooden lid. He carefully moved the items around inside, then reached to the very bottom. "Your ma wrote me a letter on that day. She said I should hear what it says someday after you were grown. I have been scared all these years of what it might tell me. I watched her cry as she wrote it. I already know she blames me for not bringing the doctor quick enough. I know everything was my fault. I kept her last words tucked away, figuring they must be real bad if she couldn't just tell me herself. She knew that I couldn't read or write. Maybe she thought I would learn someday." He solemnly handed Ethan a folded paper with writing on both sides.

"You want me to read it to you now, Pa?" Ethan asked uncertainly. He had not seen his father this distressed before, and he certainly did not want to make it worse.

John Smith took a deep breath and lowered himself onto the chair across from Ethan. "I think it's time I hear what she says. That night the old stable caught fire, I was afraid her words to me would get lost forever. Perhaps I should not have waited this long. Just read it to me and keep reading, no matter how bad it gets. I deserve what she says about me."

Ethan unfolded the letter and began to skim the page. He suddenly felt the hair on his neck standing up and chills running down his back and arms. Ethan abruptly turned the letter to see the other side. The color drained from his face as he continued to read in silence. He felt as though time had stopped, and he could not be sure if he was even breathing.

"What is it?" his father pleaded in an anguished voice. "I knew it must be bad! I knew I never deserved her love!"

Ethan did not hear anything his father said. The words on the page blurred together in front of his eyes. He was in another time and another place, in a world where their lives could never be the same. He finally snapped out of it to the cries of his father, who was now weeping uncontrollably as he stood up to leave the room. "Pa, wait!" Ethan told him quickly. "Ma never blamed you—it was never your fault! She didn't want you to feel bad for any of it!"

John Smith clutched his chest and held onto the back of a chair before he crumpled to the floor. "Why did you not just tell me, Son?" he cried in agony. "I was ready to die!"

Ethan could feel his heart pounding once more. "Pa, this letter—it's not what you think it is. It's not what you think at all."

CHAPTER 4

The next afternoon, Clara went into the library where her mother was going through the accounts. "I want a motor car," Clara declared abruptly.

Mrs. Price looked up from the ledger. She felt sorry for her daughter's broken heart, but was not about to mention the subject. She was curious about what had happened between Clara and Phillip, as any mother would be. "Very well, Child. I am certain we can arrange the purchase of a motor car at the end of the year."

"I do not want to wait that long. Can't I buy one now?" Clara asked impatiently.

"Much of your income has gone to your wardrobe. There is no money now, but if you are frugal in the coming months, you should be able to buy a car."

"When is Mary getting one?" Clara asked with a scowl.

"I expect it will be this week," answered Mrs. Price.

"I don't see why Mary should have a car when I have to keep waiting."

"Miss Mary manages her money differently than you. She has been planning this purchase for some time."

"I don't see how I can be so poor when I have received a great inheritance. Perhaps I will sell land from the estate and buy a car with the money," Clara suggested. "I can't stand to be in this miserable house another second."

"I do not think it is wise to sell now, Child. The land is what brings your income," Mrs. Price replied.

"I am not a child, and the land is not bringing income soon enough!" Clara cried angrily, storming away from the library in a huff. Mrs. Price sat bewildered at the desk, wondering exactly what had happened between the neighbor and her daughter.

Ethan and John Smith were not at the dinner table that night, and no one had seen Clara since her outburst in the library. Abigail, Mary, and Mrs. Price dined silently. "I wonder why Ethan is not at dinner tonight?" Mary thought aloud. "Did you see him today, Abigail?"

Abigail shook her head. "I have not seen him," she answered quietly. She had gone to the stable several times that day, but Ethan was nowhere in sight. Abigail worried now more than ever that Ethan's father must have objected to her, and that Ethan must not want to tell her.

Mary sat quietly, thinking of William and wishing that she had an excuse to telephone the clinic and speak to him once more. She hoped that he would call at any moment to tell her that the outbreak was over and that it was safe to visit him at the clinic. Mary noticed that her heart would ache with every hour that she waited for the phone to ring. She wondered if other families who had telephones ever felt this way. The ladies retired to bed that night with much to occupy their thoughts.

Abigail walked to the stable the next morning after

breakfast. When she still did not see Ethan, she took a deep breath and walked up the stairs to the apartment above. She was just about to knock when she noticed a paper held against the doorstop with a stone. She picked up the paper and read the words on the page.

Miss Mary,

My pa and I are not feeling well. It might be a few days before we return to work. I am sorry.

Ethan

Abigail suddenly felt guilty for assuming that Ethan did not want to see her. Now she was worried for his health. She took the letter back to the house to show Mary, who furrowed her brow at the message. "How strange. I do not think that either of them has taken a day off for sickness before."

"Then, this is the first time? I hope they are alright," remarked Abigail.

"Oh dear, what if they have the fever that William warned us about? I should telephone the clinic now." Mary went to the library telephone and told the number to the operator. Abigail stood close by. When William's voice responded on the other end, Mary felt her heart fall into her stomach. "I am afraid that Ethan and his father have fallen ill," she began. "Is there anything we can do for them?"

"Mary," William's voice said seriously. "Is anyone else at the house sick?"

"Not one of us," Mary answered.

William sighed in relief. "The outbreak in town has

been unpredictable. Just when I think that the fevers are fading, a new batch of patients arrive. I can't trace where it is coming from. You must see to it that Ethan and John get clean food and water. The fever here is typhoid, I am sure of it. Call me if they get any worse or if anyone else gets sick, alright Mary?" His voice was low and weary, sounding as if he had not slept in days.

"Yes, I will telephone if they become worse. I hope you find the source," said Mary.

"So do I. Mary, I must tell you goodbye now. I see more people walking into the clinic." And with that, their conversation was over.

Abigail heard what William had said over the telephone and began to panic. Tears ran down her cheeks as she thought about Ethan. She remembered the dreadful typhoid outbreaks in Johnstown and how many had perished from the fever. "I will deliver meals to the apartment for them," Abigail told Mary. "They must keep eating and drinking or they will lose their strength." Abigail then went to the kitchen to explain to Catherine.

"Typhoid!" the red-faced cook exclaimed. "It ain't from my cooking! I ain't no Typhoid Mary!"

"No one has suspected you of being a Typhoid Mary. I only wanted to tell you of what is happening in town before you purchase more items for the kitchen," Abigail said gently, trying to calm the high-strung cook.

"I see. Well, as long as you know it ain't because of me. I made the cakes you asked for today," Catherine replied reluctantly.

"Thank you, Catherine. You have reminded me that today is a little girl's birthday," said Abigail. She was grateful that she had something to do that would take her mind off of her worries over Ethan. Abigail arranged the cakes in a basket and included a large pink bow for Gabriella's hair. She did not want to mention to Clara that she was going to visit the Valentis that day. She felt badly for the poor family and hoped to bring them a small amount of cheer for Gabriella's birthday.

After Abigail left for the Valentis' farmhouse, Clara quietly let herself into the library. She saw the newspaper on the desk and began to browse the classifieds. She found what she was looking for.

WANTED—LAND YORK COUNTY

Paying top dollar for farmland.

Sharp Agency Phone 555-Y

Clara went to the telephone and picked up the receiver, thinking about how thrilling the first ride in her own motor car would be, once she could purchase one from the sale of her land.

Abigail knocked on the door of the Valentis' farmhouse. She was surprised when a woman answered the door. "May I help you, Miss?" asked the woman.

"Good afternoon. I am Abigail from Davenport House. I have brought a gift for Gabriella's birthday," she answered.

"Miss Abigail?" called Phillip's voice from behind the woman. He seemed amazed that Abigail was there.

Abigail smiled. "Good afternoon, Phillip."

Phillip walked out to greet her. "Allow me to introduce

my sister, Serena. She has just come from Pittsburgh to help me with the little ones while I look for work."

"I am pleased to meet you, Serena," said Abigail.

"I am pleased to meet you, Miss," replied Serena quietly. "The children are just sleeping now."

"Oh, I am sorry," whispered Abigail. "Please take this for your family to enjoy. Goodbye, Serena, Phillip." Abigail handed them the basket and turned to head back to Davenport House.

"Abigail, just a moment, please," called Phillip from behind her. She turned around to face Phillip while he closed the door to the farmhouse behind him. "I am surprised to see you. I did not expect that I would see anyone from the great house again. I imagine that Clara has told you by now…" Abigail looked embarrassed and nodded in response. Phillip tried to smile. "It was good of you to come today with the gifts. I have not forgotten your kindness, and I am glad that you still consider us friends."

Abigail nodded again. "Phillip?" she began quietly. "I just want to tell you that…I understand."

He looked into her eyes hopefully. "You do?"

"I understand what families like yours and mine have gone through. My mother warned me about being public with our faith. Although, with a surname of O'Connell and ten brothers and sisters, one could hardly wonder about me."

"Then you are Irish Catholic," Phillip Valenti chuckled. "You and I are not supposed to get along with each other, you know."

Abigail giggled. "It is why I did not tell you my surname when we first met. But I am not worried anymore."

"It is good to hear you say these words," Phillip smiled. "Thank you."

A man riding on horseback could be seen approaching the farmhouse just then. Abigail was astonished to see a familiar face from her past. "Father Salvestro!" she exclaimed happily.

The priest was an elderly man with kind eyes and a gentle demeanor. He was just as surprised to see Abigail as she was to see him. "Abigail," Father Salvestro greeted warmly. "I nearly did not recognize you. I am happy to see you looking so well."

Abigail blushed at his remark. She realized that she must look quite different from when he knew her last—a poor girl in a shantytown where the immigrants were known to live. The priest had been generous to Abigail's family and would bring them bread and sometimes gifts for Christmas. Today, Abigail wore an elegant pink afternoon dress and costly pearl necklace, her hair gracefully styled above her neck. "I am doing very well," she responded. "I have been fortunate to gain the favor of a lady who has made me her companion. Are you visiting Yorktown?"

"I have relocated. I live just down this road now," Father Salvestro explained.

"Oh my, then we are practically neighbors! I live just to the north at Davenport House."

"Then I hope that I may see you often. I heard that Gabriella has a birthday and I found a dress that looks to be her size," Father Salvestro explained.

"The children are sleeping just now. I will take the dress to the house if you wish, so that you may speak with Mr.

Valenti," Abigail offered, suddenly aware that she was keeping Phillip from his guest.

"Thank you, Child," Father Salvestro replied. Abigail took the dress from him and went to the house while Phillip stayed to talk with the priest.

"Abigail is a wonderful young lady," Father Salvestro told Phillip. "My heart is glad to see the fine choice you have made for a wife."

"Oh—um—Father—" Phillip stammered. "I am sorry to say that it was not Abigail who I was going to marry. It was another lady at the house, but she lately had a change of heart. There will be no wedding."

"I am sorry to hear that," the priest said kindly. "Forgive me for speaking out of turn."

After she left the dress with Serena, Abigail approached Phillip and Father Salvestro to say goodbye. "I must be returning to the house now," she said. "I hope I will see you again, Father. Goodbye, Phillip." The two men quietly watched Abigail walk away.

A shiny black motor car that Abigail had never seen before was parked in the drive when she returned to the house. A smartly dressed man stood near the car and appeared to be looking for someone. Abigail felt awkward as she approached. The man heard her coming and turned around to face her. "Good afternoon," he greeted, tipping his hat. "Are you Miss Clara Davenport?"

"I am not, Sir. Would you like me to announce your arrival for Clara?"

The man looked her up and down. "She told me over the telephone that she would meet me outside the house," he replied. As he was speaking, Clara emerged through the front door.

"Good afternoon, Mr. Sharp," she greeted pleasantly. Abigail felt uncomfortable standing there, so she excused herself to go into the house.

Franklin Sharp eyed Clara like she was a bakery display. "Aren't you a pretty lady," he commented, winking at her.

Clara was startled by his remark. "Thank you, Sir. Would you like to have a look at the estate?"

"Don't have to. I've already seen the maps. I will give you top dollar on the acreage. Eight thousand dollars for all five hundred."

Clara covered her heart with her hand. She had never heard of so large a sum of money in all her life. She tried to appear composed but she could barely breathe at the thought of being rich so quickly. "Mr. Sharp—I did not intend on selling my entire estate. Perhaps one hundred acres for two thousand dollars." She could hardly believe that she was negotiating with a real estate man.

"I am sorry, Miss Davenport, but that is my final offer. I have already written a Bill of Sale and have the money here in this envelope. Take it or leave it," Franklin Sharp said confidently.

Clara felt nervous as she looked at the envelope full of money. She did not want to sell all of her land, but was worried that this may be her only chance. "I might ask my mother what she thinks before I decide."

Franklin Sharp shrugged. "I am on my way to look at another parcel now. My offer to you only lasts as long as I stand here."

Clara could hear her heart pounding in her ears. She suddenly felt frightened that she must make the decision now or risk losing the offer forever.

"Suit yourself," Franklin said as he climbed into the driver's seat of the car.

"Wait!" cried Clara. "I will agree to your price, on the condition that you assist me with the purchasing of a motor car and hiring of a chauffeur. I do not know how to do so on my own."

Franklin Sharp grinned widely. "I can arrange it. Just need your signature here, Miss Davenport."

After seeing Clara with the stranger outside, Abigail went up the grand staircase and knocked on Mary's bedroom door. "Mary, there is something I must speak to you about," she said anxiously as she walked inside.

"What is it?" Mary asked in surprise.

"Has Clara explained to you why she will not marry Phillip?"

"I don't think she has left her room or spoken to anyone. I am worried that she is sore at me," Mary replied. "Even though I do not know why she would be."

"I have just seen Clara meeting with a man outside," said Abigail.

"What man? Why wasn't he announced?"

"I do not know who he is. He told me that Clara telephoned him and instructed that he should meet her in front of the house."

"How curious. I was not aware that Clara had left her room. I am certain she will explain to us later. Is that all you wished to tell me?" asked Mary.

"It is not what I came to tell you at all," Abigail sighed

and sat on a chair near Mary's bed. "Clara said that she will not marry Phillip because he is Catholic."

Mary gasped. "No wonder she has been upset! I cannot imagine what such a revelation must have been like for her."

Abigail looked at her sorrowfully. "But Mary…I am also Catholic."

Mary stared in disbelief. "It cannot be possible. You are nothing like a Catholic. My mother has told me of the dreadful things they have done. You are a good person."

"It is true that I am Catholic. Phillip is also a good person, Mary. You may not believe some of the terrible things I have heard about Protestants…but I know that you would never do such things," replied Abigail.

Mary took a deep breath. "Does Ethan know?"

Abigail shook her head sadly. "I did not think to tell him before. Then all of this happened with Clara and Phillip, and I have been in agony over whether Ethan will still want to marry me."

Mary walked over to put her arms around Abigail. "I am sorry that I reacted poorly just now. I can see how worried you are to tell Ethan." Mary paused for a moment to think. "Do you think that he will convert?" she whispered.

"I was never going to ask him to. I love him and want to be his wife. I know that I must tell him as soon as possible, but I do not know when he will be well enough to hear what I have to say," Abigail explained in despair.

"Perhaps I may tell him for you when he recovers. It may be easier coming from me," offered Mary.

Abigail tried to smile. "Thank you, Mary. If he no longer wishes to marry me, then I am afraid that I might die."

CHAPTER 5

The next morning after breakfast, Fiona announced Phillip Valenti's arrival from the Hall. Mrs. Price raised her eyebrow. She was not feeling favorable toward Phillip now that he was not marrying her daughter. Mrs. Price was still unaware of the reason. She approached Phillip and looked at him sternly.

"Good morning, Madam," he greeted nervously.

"Why have you come here? I do not believe that Clara will see you."

"I have come to speak with Miss Mary," he answered quietly. Mrs. Price hid her surprise and quietly walked away.

Mary met with Phillip in the drawing room. She did not know him very well and was confused why he would come to see her today. "What may I do for you, Mr. Valenti?"

"I have heard that you are needing a chauffeur," he started. "I am looking for work and I wish to be considered for the position."

"Oh, I see. I do not have the automobile yet. I am having trouble arranging it all because the carriage horses will be sold soon." Mary sat thoughtfully for a moment, her mind planning a solution. "Perhaps I do have work for you. Truthfully, I feel awkward asking because of your recent falling out with my sister. I do not know any other way to accomplish it, though."

"I am sure that I can manage whatever it is for you, Miss Mary. I plan to make myself scarce around Clara," he mentioned.

"Wait here a moment, please." Mary briefly left the room and returned with a paper and envelope. "I would like for you to purchase an automobile for us. Our carriage driver will take you, then you may drive the car back to the house. Here is an advertisement for the car I would like. It is the same as my friend Nellie has. I have here seven hundred dollars." Mary was hesitant to hand such a large amount of money to someone she did not know well. Abigail had called Phillip a good man, and Mary relied on that reference while she held out the envelope. "How soon will you be able to leave?"

"I can leave this minute, if you wish," Phillip replied eagerly.

Mary sighed in relief. "Very well. I will order the carriage for you now. I must tell Peter Ross that this will be his last drive for us. As for the position of chauffeur for our household, Mr. Valenti, I must consult with my sister before I make a decision. I want to be sure there is no trouble with Clara."

Abigail took a tray of dinner to Ethan and his father as she had done in the two days before. She still had not seen them since she found the note on their doorstep, and neither of the men had answered when Abigail knocked at the door. She would have been more concerned if the plates she delivered the other nights were not cleaned and stacked neatly in front of the door the following day. She laid the dinner tray on the landing and began to collect the other tray with the clean dishes. The door slowly opened in front of her.

"Oh, good evening, Mr. Smith," she said in surprise. "I have brought dinner for you." She stood up with the new dinner tray.

"Thank you, Young Lady. You have been kind to see to it that we receive food from the kitchen," he answered quietly. Abigail observed that he looked tired and had dark circles under his eyes, but he did not appear to be suffering from typhoid.

"Is Ethan alright?" she asked him.

"Why don't you see him for yourself," John Smith answered while opening the door for her. He led her to the open door of Ethan's bedroom, then turned to walk away. Abigail could see Ethan lying on the floor asleep. She carefully walked toward him and knelt down to the floor beside him. She leaned forward to press the back of her hand to his forehead. She gasped as she suddenly felt his arms slide around her waist and pull her closer to him.

Abigail could now see that although Ethan's eyes were closed, his lips were curved in a smile. Abigail giggled as she pulled herself back to a sitting position. "Then you cannot be so very ill after all," she remarked.

Ethan opened his eyes and looked up at her, grateful to see her pretty face. "You look like an angel," he told her. "I missed you."

Abigail smiled and blushed. "I missed you as well. I must speak to you when you are recovered," she said quietly.

"Oh Abigail, I was never ill in the first place," he admitted.

She gasped. "What do you mean? You had me and everyone at the house worried sick!" she scolded. "There is typhoid fever in town, and we were afraid you had it, too."

"I am sorry to worry you. I have not been able to face anyone after what I learned about my family. If we are to be married, there are things you need to know," he said seriously.

" 'If' we are to be married? Have you changed your mind?" she asked in a panic.

"No, of course not," he answered, forcing a smile. Ethan sat up from the floor and faced Abigail, looking into her eyes intently. He reached up and she soon felt the warmth of his hand against her cheek. "I wish we were married right now," he whispered.

Abigail took a deep breath. Her stomach twisted in knots while her heart fluttered from his touch. "I must tell you something about me. I do not hold the same faith as you."

"You don't?" he asked in surprise.

"No, I am Catholic. I am not allowed to marry a non-Catholic in my church, but if you still wish to marry me, we may have your minister be the one to marry us," she answered quickly.

Ethan smiled. "We can have whatever sort of wedding you would like," he said gently.

Abigail breathed in relief. "Truly? Then you do not mind?"

Ethan shook his head. "Just tell me what to do and I will be there."

"What about your pa?" she whispered. "Would he mind terribly?"

"It is fine with me, Young Lady," called John Smith's voice from the sitting room.

Abigail giggled. Her future father-in-law never seemed to miss a thing. "Oh goodness, I cannot believe that I was so worried for no reason. The truth is, I am afraid to have a ceremony where everyone will be looking at me. I would rather get married in a quiet setting."

"I would too," Ethan agreed with a smile. "But now I have something to tell you. Wait here a moment." Ethan left briefly and returned with a paper in his hand. "Pa showed me this letter just days ago. It was written by my mother. We had never read it before now. You should see it, and perhaps you can help me understand what should be done about it." Abigail gently took the paper from him and began to read.

Mary was pleased when Phillip Valenti drove up to house in a shiny black Maxwell just before dinner. She clasped her hands together in delight. "Oh, it is marvelous! I cannot believe that it belongs to me!"

Phillip smiled at her. "Peter Ross should be along in a few hours," he said. "I am glad the car meets with your expectations, Miss Mary."

"It does indeed. I cannot wait to show William. If it was safe to see him at the clinic, I would leave this instant!" she cried happily.

Clara exited the front door of the house to see what the commotion was about. When she observed that Phillip was there, she awkwardly stood at a distance. "You decided to take the chauffeur position after all," she remarked in a kinder tone than Phillip or Mary were expecting.

"I did," Phillip replied nervously. "If you are not agree-able to it—"

"Oh, do not worry about any of that," Clara interrupted

with a wave of her hand. "I am quite recovered. In fact, I will be getting a motor car with my own chauffeur. You need not worry about driving me anywhere." Clara nodded toward Mary and went back into the house. Mary was surprised to see her sister seeming sociable once more.

In the servants' quarters, Mrs. Price approached Fiona about the change in staff. "Peter Ross will be leaving in the morning as his employment has come to an end. I have decided to take an upstairs room to be closer to my daughter. With only female staff remaining in the servants' quarters, I do not feel that it is necessary for me to keep my room here to watch over you. You may have my old room after I move my things tomorrow," she explained. "You need not share with Bridget any longer."

Fiona was pleased with this news. She never had her own room before, and Mrs. Price's was more spacious than the room Fiona now shared with her sister. She went to find Bridget.

"I have good news for you," Fiona said to Bridget. "Mrs. Price is moving upstairs and I will move into the housekeeper's quarters. You will have your own room, and I will have mine!"

"How wonderful! I wonder if Mother would believe that we each have a room to ourselves here," she giggled. "We should write to her at once."

Abigail was not at the dinner table that night. Mrs. Price, Mary, and Clara dined quietly. It was Mrs. Price who finally broke the silence. "I have arranged to have my things moved to an upstairs bedroom near you, Clara," she announced with a smile. "Peter Ross leaves tomorrow."

"This is marvelous news, Mother! I was wondering

how much longer you could stand living in the stuffy servants' quarters. You will love it upstairs. I—I would like to announce my news as well," Clara stammered. "I am getting a new automobile, just like Mary. I have already arranged it."

Mrs. Price raised her eyebrows. "Whom did you arrange it with?"

"Oh Mother, you need not concern yourself with my affairs any longer. I have sold my land and will manage things myself from now on," Clara answered casually.

Mary and Mrs. Price looked at her in disbelief. "You have sold your land?" Mary asked, thinking she cannot have heard Clara correctly.

"Yes. All of it," Clara answered proudly. "As part of our business transaction, the agent has promised to send a chauffeur to the house with my new car. I cannot wait for it to arrive!"

Mrs. Price held her breath. "I hope that you did not accept a penny less than twenty thousand," she said to Clara solemnly.

Clara appeared bewildered and did not answer. She looked down at her plate and suddenly felt that she had no appetite. "I am glad to have the money more than the land," she replied quietly. Mary and Mrs. Price did not know what to say after that, and the meal was finished in silence.

Abigail was still at the apartment above the stable. She paced back and forth in the small sitting room, wringing her hands in distress. Ethan and his father were seated there and watched her quietly.

"Now you see why I could not see anyone at the house," Ethan remarked. "Should I put the letter into the fire?"

Abigail stopped in her tracks. "No!" she cried suddenly. "You cannot think of doing such a thing."

"Then what should I do?" he pleaded. "If she discovers the truth, it will change everything. I could never forgive myself for taking away everything she's ever known."

Abigail looked sorrowful. "There is no simple answer to this. But Mary must be made aware at the very least. Perhaps we may leave the decision with her of what she will do with the information. If anyone else is to know, it must be she who tells it."

Ethan nodded. "Which of us should tell her?"

Abigail took a deep breath. "The words would be impossible for me to utter. Come to the house first thing in the morning. We will tell Mary in her room, away from the others. I must return to the house now. I do not know how I will sleep tonight."

"We won't be sleeping either," remarked John Smith. But even in his weary voice, there seemed to be a tone of relief, as if the heaviness he usually carried had somehow been lessened. Although Abigail had told them that she intended to return to the house, she continued to pace the room in front of Ethan and his father before finally settling down into a chair. She looked at the both of them in amazement, but no one said another word about it for the rest of the evening.

Clara retired to her room after dinner. Mary met Mrs. Price in the drawing room for tea. They watched the fire in the grand marble fireplace. "I am sorry for what my daughter has done, Miss Mary," Mrs. Price apologized.

"I am afraid that I share the blame in this. I had considered placing Clara's land into a trust instead of directly transferring the deeds. It was too much for her…I should have known better."

"I hope the new owner is gracious to the tenants," Mrs. Price remarked.

"I nearly fainted when Clara said that she has sold it all. Does she plan to live elsewhere?" asked Mary.

"My daughter does not share her plans with me," replied Mrs. Price.

Mary sighed. "Perhaps when she finds that she regrets the sale, I might place twenty acres of my estate into trust for her. My father used to emphasize the importance of having land to fall back on."

"You have already been generous to us when we never deserved it. Thank you, Miss Mary," Mrs. Price said emotionally.

Mary managed a smile. "I believe it is what my father would have wanted. I hope that he is watching me now and is pleased with what I have done."

Chapter 6

The next morning, Mary was at her vanity table staring blankly at her reflection in the mirror. She wondered if she should telephone William before breakfast, or if it would be a bad time at the clinic. If it was a bad time, she did not know when a good time would be. As she was pondering this, Bridget walked into her room with a breakfast tray. "Good morning, Miss," she greeted, setting the tray on the table.

"Good morning, Bridget. Why have you brought me a tray? I was just about to leave for the dining room," Mary said confused.

"Oh—you did not wish to have breakfast in your room?" asked Bridget. "Forgive me, Miss Mary, I was told to bring you a tray today."

"Told by whom?" questioned Mary.

"Miss Abigail," replied Bridget. "I will take it back to the kitchen if it was a misunderstanding."

Mary heard a loud ringing sound coming from downstairs just then. She forgot about everything else and hurried out of the room. Mary held onto the rail as she ran down the grand staircase, thinking that any moment she might trip and fall. She made it to the library just as Fiona was answering the telephone.

"Dr. Hamilton to speak with you, Miss Mary," Fiona announced, holding the receiver in her hand.

Mary eagerly took it from Fiona and spoke into the telephone. "William?"

"Good morning, Mary," his voice answered cheerfully.

Mary sighed in relief. "Good morning! Is it safe to come to town now?" It was the only question she had.

"I believe so. The cases of fever have subsided. I never did find the source, but our last patient leaves today. I thought you might like to know. Have Ethan and John recovered?"

"I am not certain. I have not seen either of them, but Abigail has reported that they have eaten heartily this week," Mary replied.

"I am glad to hear it. You have reminded me of how delicious the dinners are at Davenport House…" he trailed off.

Mary smiled. "Do you wish to join us for dinner?" she asked excitedly.

William laughed. "I cannot tell you how much I have longed to hear those words. I will see you tonight, Mary. I can't wait. Goodbye for now."

"Goodbye," Mary responded. She placed the receiver into the cradle and covered her red cheeks with her hands. She thought about what jewelry she might wear tonight that could help her dreary black dress appear more cheerful.

Abigail entered the library just then. Mary told her the good news from William, but Abigail looked pale and distressed, as if the news meant nothing to her. "Mary—I have asked for your breakfast to be sent to your room today. There is a serious matter that we must discuss. In your room."

Mary was confused, but went to her bedroom with Abigail. Mary was stunned to find Ethan waiting for her inside. "You look well!" she exclaimed in relief, but then began to panic. "Has something happened to your pa?"

"No, Miss Mary. We are well," he answered quietly, trying to swallow the lump in his throat. "We were never ill. I am sorry to have worried you."

"I don't understand," Mary responded. "What is happening? Why have you come to meet me here?"

Ethan stared at her in silence. He had been staring ever since Mary walked through the door. Abigail watched the two of them and finally spoke. "There is something you must see, Mary" she said gently. Abigail nodded toward Ethan to proceed.

Ethan took a deep breath and removed a folded paper from his pocket. "It is a letter. Pa never showed me until now. We didn't know what to do at first, but now…it belongs to you," He handed the paper to Mary with shaking hands.

Mary sat down on her bed and glanced at the first line. "I don't understand. This is not addressed to me," she remarked, looking up at Ethan and Abigail.

"You should brace yourself, Mary," warned Abigail. "Read to the end." Mary returned her gaze to the letter. She appeared confused at first, then held her breath until she had read every last word. Ethan rushed to Mary's side as her eyes appeared to roll back and her body began to fall forward.

Ethan caught her and lifted her gently upon the bed. Abigail began to cry and covered her face with her hands.

"Tell me that we did the right thing to show her!" Ethan cried.

Abigail looked at him helplessly. "I do not know!"

It was Peter Ross's last day of employment at Davenport House. Mrs. Price collected the money from the sale of the horses and sent Peter away with his final wages.

"You have served our house faithfully for years, Mr. Ross. I am sorry to see you go," Mrs. Price said kindly.

"I thank you for the additional wage you are sending with me. I expect I will go West now where most folks still have horses," Mr. Ross replied quietly.

"I wish you all the best," she said to him.

Mary had approved of Peter Ross being driven to the train station in the new car to begin the next chapter of his life. He gratefully climbed into the seat beside Phillip and they drove to town.

Mrs. Price went into the house to admire her new upstairs bedroom. Soft lace curtains graced the windows while filtered light flowed in from the outside, creating delicate patterns that danced on the walls. The bed was soft and luxurious. Mrs. Price thought about the days gone by when she was only a young woman engaged to a wealthy man. She had worked as a housemaid for the Davenport family, and eventually fell in love with the eldest son, James. He always treated her and the rest of the staff with kindness.

Mrs. Price recalled how she and James planned to elope until a jealous woman sabotaged their union. The room that Mrs. Price now chose to be her upstairs room had always been her favorite in the house. She would often dream of how she might have lived in the delightful room all this while if only James had married her as he promised. Mrs. Price would have been the Mistress of Davenport House, had it not been for the plots of a deceitful woman named Margaret.

When Mrs. Price was still a housemaid, she and James conceived a child during their secret engagement. Margaret was a beautiful Irish lady who was shrewd in business as well as romantic attachments. Her parents were acquaintances of the Davenports and Margaret had set her sights on James from a young age. Although Mrs. Price never told a soul of the pregnancy, Margaret found out and declared at the dinner table that the Davenport's housemaid was with child. Mrs. Price was dismissed immediately. She wrote many letters to James, asking when they would finally marry. But Margaret had gotten to James before the marriage could take place. Margaret convinced him that a servant was the child's true father. James soon married Margaret, but could not forget his first love. He allowed Mrs. Price to work in the new house in York County, where their daughter Clara was born. Mrs. Price always hoped that someday, her daughter might be recognized for who she truly was.

Clara was in her bedroom, counting the money in the envelope over and over. She placed five hundred dollars into the purse that she would bring with her for shopping. She worried over whether she could have sold the land for more money as her mother had suggested. Clara wondered if the amount that her mother had mentioned could have truly been obtained, or if her mother was only trying to shame her for selling her estate. Clara could hear a car driving toward the house just then. She looked at the drive from her bedroom window and gasped.

"My automobile is here!" she squealed. She hurried down the grand staircase and out the front door. Fiona was already on her way to the door to greet the visitor. "It is my new car," Clara told her. "Let us meet my chauffeur!" Clara led the way while Fiona followed.

"Are you Miss Davenport?" asked the driver.

"I am," she answered proudly. "And you are?"

"The name's Stuart. Mr. Sharp sent me with your car. Is it to your liking, Miss?"

"It is!" Clara exclaimed as she clasped her hands together in delight. "This is Fiona, our housekeeper. She will inform you when I need to order the car in the future." Stuart nodded and winked at Fiona when Clara was not looking. Fiona looked at the ground and wanted to go back into the house.

"I wish to leave for Philadelphia right away," Clara said. "I have shopping to do." Stuart helped Clara climb into the car and they were soon on their way. Fiona went back into the house feeling strange about the man she just met.

After Mrs. Price settled into her new room, she went to look for her daughter all throughout the house. She suddenly realized that she had not seen Mary, Clara, or Abigail that day. Mrs. Price dined alone at lunchtime and wondered where the girls could be.

Mary slowly opened her eyes. The room appeared blurry at first, but she could soon see Ethan sitting on the floor beside the bed, appearing to be deep in thought.

Abigail was not in the room. "Is it true?" Mary whispered to Ethan. "Or have I only dreamed it?"

Ethan looked up at her. "I am still trying to understand it, myself," he replied. "Abigail has left to order tea for us."

"Was your father really in prison?" Mary questioned.

Ethan nodded. "He told me just days ago. He said he worked for the wrong people and got arrested. I could not believe it at first, but after I read the letter...I have never been so shocked in my life."

"Does anyone else know of the letter?"

"Only Abigail...and Pa."

"What does he say?"

"He has hardly spoken of it, Miss Mary," answered Ethan.

"Where is the letter?" Mary asked, sitting up in bed and looking around the room. "I wish to read it again."

In the servants' quarters, Fiona was proudly showing her new room to Bridget. "Can you believe my lovely room has its own desk? It is so spacious. I even have a tea table. You and I may take our tea in here like real ladies."

"The room is lovely," said Bridget quietly. "Fiona, something is troubling me."

"What is it?"

"I thought that Miss Abigail was engaged—to the stable boy," began Bridget.

"She is, as far as I know," Fiona replied.

"But I watched him enter Miss Mary's room this morning. I have just taken tea to her room, and he was still there. Miss Mary was lying on the bed. They have been alone all day," Bridget said worriedly.

Fiona's eyes were wide. "I would not believe such a thing

if it did not come from you just now. Perhaps there is an explanation. Miss Mary is too proper for an indiscretion."

"But Miss Abigail is so kind," Bridget said with tears in her eyes. "She understands us because she is Irish like we are. Remember how she showed compassion to you and me when we first trained to be housemaids here? She often asks about how our family is faring in Yorktown, but now I am the one who is worried for her."

Fiona gently placed her hand on her sister's shoulder. "I understand that you are worried. But we are servants, and this is not our business. We must leave it to the family to do as they will."

Bridget nodded. "I do hope there is an explanation. Miss Abigail has shown me the beautiful wedding dress that she will wear. I helped her to try it on. I only wish for her to be happy, always."

Abigail found Mrs. Price in the library. "Mary wishes to see you in her room, Mrs. Price," she said solemnly.

"Oh?" asked Mrs. Price in surprise. "Is everything alright? I have not seen any of you girls all day."

"I wish that I could say everything is alright," replied Abigail.

"Is Clara with Miss Mary?" asked Mrs. Price, rising from her seat.

"She is not. I have not seen Clara today," answered Abigail. She and Mrs. Price left the library and headed for the grand staircase.

Mrs. Price observed Fiona in the Hall. "Fiona, has Clara come out of her room today?"

"She has gone to Philadelphia, Mrs. Price," answered Fiona.

Mrs. Price was stunned. "I don't understand," she said in disbelief.

"Miss Clara's new motor car arrived today and she instructed the driver to take her to Philadelphia."

"She has gone away with Phillip?" asked Mrs. Price.

"No, Mrs. Price. Miss Clara now has a chauffeur called Stuart."

Mrs. Price sighed. "Thank you, Fiona. Please notify me when my daughter returns. I must go with Abigail to Miss Mary's room now. "

Fiona's eyes grew wide. "Of course," she replied. She hoped that Mary knew they were coming.

Mrs. Price entered Mary's bedroom. She was startled to see Ethan sitting with Mary alone in the room. She looked at Abigail, then back at Mary and Ethan. Since Mrs. Price was the only one in the room who seemed shocked, she decided that something bigger must be going on—something she was about to be made aware of.

"Mrs. Price, I ask you here today because you are the only one who can verify something of a most sensitive nature," began Mary. "There is a letter that was recently discovered, and its contents must be treated with discretion."

"I see. Who has sent it?" Mrs. Price questioned.

"It was written by my mother," Ethan answered quietly. "They are her last words."

Mrs. Price's eyes widened. "The letter is from Maryanne? Where has it been all this while?"

"Just please read to the end, and tell me if you knew of any of it," answered Mary distressed.

Mrs. Price took the letter and began to read. The look of dismay in her countenance told the others that the

contents were as shocking to her as they were to everyone else.

Dearest Anna,

*I pray this letter reaches you one day, when you are
the fine lady you always deserved to be. Your father
worries that he is to blame for not going for the doctor
sooner, but it was never his fault. The doctor will not
come for me, for he knows my secret and he wishes
for the truth to die with me. When your father was
imprisoned, I was poor and starving with no way to
care for you. That was when the doctor found me. He
said that an important lady would raise you in a grand
house and that you would want for nothing. I could
not give you up, but the doctor took you from me at
my weakest moment and instructed the nurse to leave
me to die. The nurse would not obey the doctor, and
helped me to find you. I arrived at Davenport House
the next day and pleaded with the housekeeper to hire
me as a nurse for the newborn baby. Mrs. Price showed
pity on me when I convinced her that my own baby
had died and that I had milk to nurse another. I was
hired that moment, and neither Margaret nor anyone
in the house knew that I was your true mother. I have
loved to be by your side and watch you grow. I love
you and your brother dearly. I know you will take care
of him after I am gone because I see how much your
heart cares for him, already knowing what your mind
does not. Tell your father that I love him and that he
has never done a thing wrong. I hid from the doctor for
years whenever he was in the house, but one day he saw*

*me. Now he refuses to help when he knows I will die.
I know I am sinning by keeping it from John that you
were not truly lost. I fear that if he discovers the doctor's
crimes, John will kill him and be hanged. I have come
to peace with your being raised in Davenport House. I
wished sometimes that I could take you away, but you
are cared for by a kind man. I could not have given you
the life that he will. I hope that my family will forgive
me for this truth I have withheld. The nurse who helped
me was called Anna. I must call you Mary in the house,
but I have named you Anna in my heart. With my last
breaths I give all my love to John, and to my children,
Anna and Ethan.*

Truly,

Your Mother

Mrs. Price looked aghast when she had read the letter to
its end. "One hears of such things happening in other great
houses—but never this one!" Mrs. Price cried in a whisper. "Although the thought of it seems impossible, it would
answer a question that has bothered me all these years."

"How do you mean?" asked Mary quickly.

Mrs. Price sighed. "After your brother Richard was
born, the Master told the Mistress that he planned to
divorce her. It was going to be a great scandal and the
Mistress was terrified. It was then that she announced she
was with child again. The other servants and I suspected
that it was a lie to fool the Master…but then the doctor
ordered her to be on bed rest for months and…she delivered you. No one questioned it again."

"Then it *is* true," Mary said with tears in her eyes. Bridget knocked on the door just then.

"Are you ready for me to attend to you, Miss Mary?" she asked through the door.

Mary's eyes were wide with fear. "Is it dinnertime already?" she thought aloud. "Come in, Bridget."

Bridget walked in and was surprised to see so many people gathered there looking serious. She worried about the conversation that must be taking place that would cause them such distress. Mary continued, "I don't believe that I will dress for dinner tonight. Please have a tray brought when it is ready."

"Very good, Miss Mary. Um...Dr. Hamilton has arrived for dinner," Bridget said hesitantly.

Mary gasped. "I had forgotten that William was coming tonight! What should I do?" she asked no one in particular.

"Bridget, will you excuse us for a moment?" Abigail asked her kindly. Bridget nodded and left the room.

"I have wanted desperately to see William. I did not think that it would be when I am in a state like this!" Mary cried.

"Perhaps we may arrange for dinner to be served for only you and William in the upstairs sitting room," offered Abigail. "We understand that you are not prepared for a formal meal."

Mary sighed. "But how will I explain this?" No one had an answer for her. Mrs. Price left to tell the staff of the change in dinner plans. Abigail left to dress for dinner. Ethan was still with Mary.

"I will go back to the stable and have dinner with Pa,"

said Ethan quietly. He went to Mary and put his arms around her. "I am sorry about all of this."

"I don't know how sorry I am, if it means that you have been my brother all this while," she replied, hugging him back. "But why did you not tell me the moment you found out?"

"I was worried for you. I thought you might not have your inheritance anymore."

"Oh dear," replied Mary. "I had not even considered. I cannot think of these things now or I will go mad. I have to see William tonight. I want to tell him everything."

"Good luck, Miss Mary," said Ethan.

Clara arrived at the house with barely enough time to change for dinner. She ordered Fiona and Bridget to carry the boxes she brought back from Philadelphia upstairs to her bedroom. Clara sighed with happiness as she dressed in one of her new evening gowns. "Did anyone miss me while I was away?" she asked Bridget, who was attending her.

Bridget smiled. "I am sure they did, Miss."

"Have you seen my new car?"

"Only from the window in the hall, Miss Clara."

"It is heavenly. I had such fun on the drive today. Next time, perhaps I will go to New York. There is much to do and see there."

"Sounds lovely, Miss," Bridget answered politely.

Clara went downstairs to the dining room. Mrs. Price, Abigail, and Ethan were there, but the room was very quiet. "Where is my sister?" asked Clara.

"Miss Mary is taking her dinner upstairs in the sitting room with Dr. Hamilton," answered Mrs. Price, hoping that Clara would not ask any more questions.

Clara giggled. "Sounds romantic. I wonder if tonight will be the night?"

"What night?" asked Mrs. Price.

"When William asks for her hand, of course," answered Clara cheerfully. "I am glad that Mary is seeing William once more. She has seemed terribly lonely this week." The room was very quiet. Clara wondered if something had happened while she was away. "Isn't anyone going to ask me where I have been all day?" she asked.

"I was surprised when Fiona said you had left for Philadelphia," Mrs. Price commented.

"I certainly did! Philadelphia was brilliant. I must confess, I do miss planning my wedding when I see all of the delightful things that may be of use. Abigail, why don't I help you plan your wedding? I am happy to take you to Philadelphia in my new car. We can shop all day."

Abigail smiled. "It is kind of you to offer, Clara. Thank you."

William was shown into the upstairs sitting room where Mary was waiting for him. A table was set with a fine linen table cloth and silver candlesticks, and the room was dimly lit by the flickering flames of the candles. Mary felt her heart flutter when William walked through the double doors. She rose from her seat and instantly felt his strong arms around her. "Mary," he whispered. "It has been too long."

Mary held onto him tightly. "It feels like ages. Thank you for coming tonight."

"What a week it has been in Yorktown," he said smiling, looking into her eyes. "I often thought of how much I wanted to come to Davenport House, where everything is beautiful."

Mary smiled even though she was sure she was

blushing. "We should begin our dinner. There is much to say tonight, but let us keep our voices down when the servants are near."

After dinner, Clara and Mrs. Price walked together up the grand staircase. "I have something to show you, Mother," said Clara. "Come to my room where you will be surprised!" Mrs. Price followed Clara into the bedroom where costly dresses were displayed hanging from the wardrobe. "You do not need to wear that old housekeeper's uniform anymore," Clara proudly told her. "Look at these lovely fashions that I picked up for you in Philadelphia."

"Oh my," Mrs. Price replied. She had never worn a fashionable thing in her life. "You are kind, Child. But when could I ever wear these? They are rather bright."

"That is the whole point," Clara said, holding up one of the dresses to her mother's figure. "Oh Mother, this one is brilliant for you! Why, you look ten years younger!"

Mrs. Price laughed. "Then it is a miracle dress. You need not spend your money on pretty things for me. I am worried that you cannot afford them."

Clara's face fell. "Do you not like the dresses, Mother?"

Mrs. Price smiled. "The dresses are nice. Perhaps they are too nice for me. I am content in my uniform dress."

Clara was disappointed. "I will hang them in your wardrobe, anyway. Then once you get used to the colors, you may decide you wish to wear one."

"Thank you, Child," replied her mother. She was sure that she would never wear one, but she appreciated the gesture just the same.

Clara had also purchased a locket necklace for her aunt who worked in the kitchen. She went down the stairs to the servants' quarters and gave the necklace to her aunt. Catherine seemed much more enthusiastic about the gift than Clara's mother had about the dresses. Satisfied with her aunt's reaction, Clara headed back upstairs. Fiona met her in the Hall.

"Miss Clara," Fiona addressed her.

"What is it?" asked Clara.

"It is about the new driver, Stuart. He says he expects room and board as part of his contract," answered Fiona.

"Oh! Well, show him into Peter Ross's old room. It is vacant, is it not?"

"It is vacant, Miss Clara," Fiona replied nervously.

"Well then, it is perfect timing. I am retiring to bed now. Goodnight."

"Goodnight, Miss Clara."

Mary and William were on the settee in the upstairs sitting room. William held the letter and was reading in bewilderment. He carefully set the letter on the end table next to him, then turned to take Mary's hands in his. He gazed at her in amazement.

"Can you believe it?" asked Mary anxiously.

"Of course I can believe it," he answered, his gaze never leaving her face. "Mary—you look just like her! The truth has been in front of me all this while, and I never thought to put the two together!"

"Do you mean it? You can see the resemblance?" Mary asked, her heart beating loudly in her chest. She often considered Ethan's mother to be the most beautiful woman she had known.

"I do mean it, truly. Oh Mary, this explains so much. Do you remember the day we met when you brought the basket to the farmhouse? I—I fell in love the moment I saw your face. I could not explain it. I always hoped that someday I would find a lady just like her. You are kind like her and you even sound like her when you speak. You are nothing like the other woman who you thought was your mother. Nothing."

Mary could hardly breathe. Never had she heard so many beautiful words together at the same time. She did not have time to think about what she might say next because William was leaning toward her, looking as though he was going to kiss her. Mary closed her eyes, and it was not much longer until she could feel his warm face against hers.

CHAPTER 7

The next morning at Davenport House, Clara had left her bedroom early. She wondered where she should journey next in her new car. She quietly walked into the library and found a fresh copy of the newspaper that had been laid on the desk. She flipped through the pages and observed a listing that immediately caught her eye.

FOR SALE-500 ACRES FARMLAND

York County, Near Davenport House.

Price: 25,000

Sharp Agency Phone 555-Y

Clara gasped and covered her mouth with her hand. Her heart felt as though it was beating in front of her and sinking into her stomach at the same time. Worried that her mother or Mary might see the listing, Clara removed the page and smoothed the newspaper neatly on the desk to look as though it had not been touched. She folded the page in her shaking hands and placed it in her dress pocket.

"Fiona?" she called as she saw Fiona walk past the double doors of the library. "Tell Stuart that I wish him to bring the car at once."

Mary sighed as she lay on her bed, staring dreamily at the ceiling. She felt that even with everything that had happened the day before, she could not stop smiling. Abigail knocked on the door and entered the room. "Good morning, Mary," she said, sounding surprised. "I wondered if you might like me to order breakfast to your room today."

Mary sat up with a smile. "Not today. I will go to the dining room. I feel quite cheerful after dinner with William last night."

"You look quite cheerful," Abigail giggled. "What did William say about it?"

"Oh…just that he can see the resemblance. William was acquainted with Mrs. Smith when he was younger. He also told me that he fell in love with me the moment we met."

Abigail gasped. "It was an eventful dinner, indeed! Perhaps I should have been there to chaperon for you," she teased.

Mary giggled. "I am glad that we had no chaperon, because then William might not have kissed me again."

Abigail laughed, then took a small pillow from the fainting couch and playfully tossed it at Mary. "Why have you been kissed *three* times now, when I am the one who is engaged, and have never been kissed at all?"

Mary laughed. "Should I have a word with my brother about it?"

"Oh Mary, I am relieved to hear you speak this way. I was so worried for how you might react to the letter."

"I was overwhelmed for certain. I did not know what

to think, but after the things that William said to me last night, I wonder if it may turn out for the better."

Clara arrived at the Sharp Agency in Yorktown. She marched into the office, holding the newspaper page in her hand and was ready to give Franklin Sharp a piece of her mind. The secretary showed Clara to Franklin's office. "Miss Clara Davenport to see you, Sir," she announced.

"Come right in, Clara," Franklin Sharp greeted cheerfully. "You are fortunate to see me before my first appointment."

"Fortunate?" she demanded. "You call this fortunate?" She slammed the page on his desk.

"My, you're a feisty one, ain't you?" he laughed.

"You tricked me!" Clara cried indignantly. "My land was worth three times what you paid! I want it back. I will buy it back from you."

"Too late for that, unless you have twenty-five thousand in that little purse of yours. Eh, you're a woman. I don't expect you to understand how business works."

Clara's mouth hung open. "It cannot be legal to do such a thing!" she persisted. "I will hire a lawyer."

"Hire a lawyer if you want, but I'll save you some trouble by telling you that what I did was legal. In America we call it 'business'. If you don't like it, you shouldn't be in business," he replied. "Now if you'll excuse me, I do have an appointment. About this very posting, as a matter of fact."

"Then I will warn your client not to deal with you! You are a snake!" Clara exclaimed.

Franklin Sharp was unaffected. He only laughed as if he found it funny to watch Clara being upset. The secretary came to the door. "Mrs. Margaret Davenport to see you, Sir."

Clara looked in horror as a tall woman in a long black dress and black gloves entered the room. It was the woman who had made Clara's life more difficult than it ever should have been. "Clara," Mrs. Davenport greeted. "I cannot say that I am surprised to see you here, considering the newspaper this morning."

"She was just leaving, Mrs. Davenport," Franklin Sharp assured her.

"No, please stay here, Clara. We may be able to help each other out," Mrs. Davenport said in a friendly tone.

"You—you want me to stay here while you speak with Mr. Sharp, Madam?" Clara could not believe her ears. She sat down before her knees buckled underneath her.

"Now tell me, Dear. How much did this snake offer you for my husband's land?" Mrs. Davenport asked her.

Clara almost felt relieved to hear Franklin called a snake by someone else, but she was also embarrassed to declare the amount she sold it for. "He offered me eight thousand, Madam," Clara answered nervously.

Mrs. Davenport turned to look at Franklin sternly. "It is the same amount that I will offer today."

"Just a minute now, Mrs. Davenport. I ain't running a charity here. I gotta make money. I have other clients who will pay at least twice that today."

"I see. And did any of your other clients see you at Mr. Schneider's Christmas Party? Perhaps with Mr. Schneider's wife?" Mrs. Davenport asked daringly.

Franklin slumped his shoulders. "I expect not."

"Interesting," Mrs. Davenport responded, pulling

a document from her handbag. "I have a Bill of Sale just here. I only need to fill in the amount which I will do now. Eight…thousand…" she said aloud as she wrote on the contract. "Take it or leave it, Franklin. You are not out a nickel from this transaction. Consider yourself fortunate."

Franklin grumbled as he signed his name to the Bill of Sale and handed it to Mrs. Davenport. "Now leave my office. I have other appointments—ones that won't waste my time."

Mrs. Davenport counted out the money for him and turned to leave. "Thank you, Clara. Why don't you walk in town with me for a moment. The shop down the way has just received a delivery of new items today."

Clara was bewildered, but wished to leave that office as soon as possible anyway. Before she knew it, she was walking past the shops with Mrs. Davenport, who seemed friendlier than usual. "I am glad you were there today," Mrs. Davenport laughed. "I nearly offered him fifteen thousand. I never dreamed you could have sold it for less."

Clara's face turned red. "I suppose I should have spoken to my mother first. She did not want me to sell at all."

"Let's face it, Clara. Your mother is a housekeeper, not a land steward. The price for farmland is at its peak now. You made the right choice to sell, only you did not know an appropriate sale price. I'm afraid that with the way your mother and Mary are running things, they will drive the estate into the ground."

"How do you mean?" asked Clara.

"The price of the land will drop soon, and the land they could have sold now will be near worthless. I don't imagine the house will be able to keep functioning in another five years the way it has in the past."

Clara looked worried. "Then we should lessen our expenses," she suggested.

"It won't be enough to merely lessen your expenses. The estate must be made sustainable with the valuable plots sold now while the price is high. Clara, do you know why the estate and house flourished while my husband was alive?" Clara shook her head. Mrs. Davenport continued, "It is because I was the land steward. With the way your mother is managing the estate, Mary will be left a pauper and the servants will be out of work. I expect it can only go another ten years at most."

Clara began to panic. "How terrible! Mary must be made aware of this right away!"

Mrs. Davenport laughed. "Mary will not listen to a thing you or I say. But if you will listen to me now, I do know of a way we may save the estate."

" 'We'?" asked Clara. "What has this to do with me?"

"There are things you do not know about Mary's past. Things that would mean that Mary should never have received an inheritance," Mrs. Davenport said mysteriously.

"I don't understand. Mary inherited everything once Richard was incarcerated," Clara replied.

"Not exactly. My husband wrote in his Will that his daughter should inherit. He did not specify Mary's name."

"But Mary was the daughter he meant, of course," Clara said.

"You are correct. However, the law will not see it that way."

Clara continued to look confused. She wondered why Mrs. Davenport was telling her these things in the first place. She was always under the impression that Mrs. Davenport hated her. "What reason could the law have to say that Mary should not inherit?"

Mrs. Davenport laughed again. "The reason is simple. Mary was never my husband's child. However, you are his child. His only daughter."

Clara looked aghast. "Who is her father?"

Mrs. Davenport shrugged. "No one knows. I took Mary in when she was an infant. Her mother was probably some wayward woman who could not care for a child. My husband and I raised Mary as our own, but she was never adopted through the court. That is why I say the law will not see her as the daughter named in the Will. Claim your inheritance, Clara. If you let me work as the land steward once more, I will see to it that your estate is well profitable."

"I could never take Mary's inheritance from her," Clara said quietly. Her head was spinning. She could not believe the conversation she was having with the woman who was once her enemy.

"How very noble of you. I understand that you wish to be loyal to Mary, but the estate will still be taken from her. It is only a matter of time. The servants will be left on the streets…you, your mother, even Mary will need to find work to make ends meet. You must not view it as taking the estate away from Mary, but rather saving it from the management that will mean its ruin."

Clara reasoned that Mrs. Davenport made a convincing argument. "But how would I prove the circumstances of Mary's birth to the trustee?"

Mrs. Davenport smiled. "That is where I come in. The

necessary documents can only come from me, and I am sure that you don't expect me to provide them for free."

"You want me to—pay you for the documents?" Clara stammered.

"My husband nearly left me destitute with an income of only one hundred dollars a year. It might as well be a servant's wage. I want five thousand dollars. Surely you have that left over from your sale."

Clara looked horrified. "Five thousand for a piece of paper? But in the agent's office, I saw that you had money in your handbag."

"I did have money in my handbag, but sadly it is not mine. I was forced to borrow from my friends just to be able to undo the mess you made with the sale," Mrs. Davenport answered bitterly.

"Oh, I see. But five thousand dollars is almost all the money I have left, Madam. I do not know that I could pay such a sum for only some documents."

Mrs. Davenport shrugged again. "You are forgetting that you could receive what is left of the estate, including the house. I will not force you to make the decision now, Clara. I am not a snake like Franklin Sharp. Just come to me when you realize that I am right. You know where to find me."

In the dining room that night, Mary, Clara, Abigail, and Mrs. Price were having dinner. Everyone seemed quiet again. Clara decided that she must speak up. "Mary, have you thought about selling land from the estate in the near future?"

Mary was surprised to hear this question from Clara. "I have discussed it with your mother, and we believe it is best to keep ownership of the land. Father used to tell me of the importance of owning land for financial security." Mary hoped that her reply did not sound snobbish, considering that Clara no longer owned any of the estate.

"Perhaps you should discuss it with your own mother," Clara remarked.

Mary was aghast at Clara's suggestion. Mary had been estranged from Mrs. Davenport and felt that Clara should have known better than to mention her now. "Why would you say that?"

"She was the land steward after all. If anyone would know when to sell and when to keep ownership, it would be her," Clara answered.

"Have you—spoken to my mother?" Mary asked in disbelief.

"I saw your mother in town. She mentioned that now is the time to sell for the best price."

Mary felt herself becoming flustered. "She is the last person I would wish to speak to about finances, Clara. I do not believe she can be trusted."

"You might be surprised, Mary. She has been kind to you over the years, perhaps even more than you know."

"I cannot listen to this anymore!" Mary cried emotionally. "I will never trust a word that comes from that woman!" Mary rose from her seat and hurried out of the dining room.

"Clara, now is not the time to speak of such things," Mrs. Price said firmly.

"I disagree. If we do not sell for a good price now, we may never have the chance again," Clara responded.

Abigail went to Mary's room to try to console her. "I

am sorry, Mary," she told her softly. "Clara does not know what she says."

"I felt so strange when Clara spoke of my mother. I know who she meant of course, but in my mind I could only think that my real mother is dead. All this time I have thought that my father was dead and my mother was living, but now I discover that it is the other way around. I am confused. I do not know what to think." Tears ran down Mary's face as she explained her thoughts. Abigail listened compassionately.

"Mary, have you spoken to Mr. Smith at all? I wonder if it might help. You may feel as though you have lost both of your parents, but there is one who remains, and he is a good man," said Abigail.

"I have been afraid to even think of doing so. What would I say? Does he even wish to see me now?" Mary continued to cry.

Abigail put her arms around Mary. "I will ask him for you, if you wish."

After the awkward dinner and disapproving glances from her mother, Clara quietly left the dining room and summoned Stuart from the servants' quarters. Clara told him that she wished to be driven to a cottage that was situated a short distance from the house. She did not wish to walk, now that she had a car to take her, but more than that she did not wish to go alone. The sky seemed darker than usual that evening as Clara approached the small cottage near the estate. Even in the dark, the structure appeared to be in need of repair, and Clara could hardly believe that a lady of an important family was living in such a house. A coyote's howl echoed mournfully in the distance, causing

Clara to jump and look around her in fright. She looked back toward the car where Stuart was waiting, but Clara could hardly see him or anything else.

The headlights illuminating the path in front of the car were nearly quenched by the surrounding darkness. Clara turned back to look at the windows of the cottage, most of which showed cracks in the glass or had been boarded up altogether. She tried to ignore the sinking feeling in her stomach and nearly lost her nerve with every step she took. Clara slowly lifted her hand to knock on the door, but froze in that position as she contemplated why she was there. She thought better of it and returned her hand to her side, abruptly turning on her heel to leave. Before Clara could break out into a run toward the car, she heard the door of the cottage creak open behind her.

"Clara," called the voice of Mrs. Davenport. "I have been expecting you."

CHAPTER 8

Clara was not at breakfast the next morning. Mary decided to make an announcement to Mrs. Price and Abigail. "I have decided that I will tell Clara today. It does not seem right to keep such a secret from her. I am doing my best to come to terms with it, myself. Although I do think this is a subject that we should only keep within the family."

Mrs. Price nodded in agreement. "I believe it is wise to do so."

"I plan to go for a ride today," Mary stated. "What do you say, Abigail? It has been so long since we took the horses out. They must worry that we forgot about them."

Abigail smiled when she thought about seeing Ethan. "I would like that very much," she answered.

Clara arrived in Yorktown at the office of the trustee who used to manage Mr. Davenport's affairs. It was he who distributed the estate to Mary after Mr. Davenport passed away. The trustee's secretary led Clara down the short hallway to Mr. Morgan's office. "Miss Clara Davenport to see you, Sir," announced the secretary.

Mr. Morgan raised his eyebrows. "Good morning, Miss. Do we have an appointment?"

"I am sorry that I did not make an appointment in advance, Mr. Morgan. I only have some documents to show you. It involves the estate of the recently deceased Mr. Davenport. You see, I am his daughter."

"You are a daughter of James Davenport?" Mr. Morgan asked in surprise. "I have already closed the estate after settling distribution on Miss Mary Davenport."

"I understand that, Mr. Morgan," Clara persisted. "But I have here a letter from his widow and an affidavit that explains how Mary was never their natural born daughter."

Mr. Morgan looked puzzled as he read the affidavit. "How peculiar. Mrs. Davenport never said a word of this when I represented the estate. Why did she not mention you at the time? Are you not her daughter also?"

"I am not, Sir. My mother—she was the housekeeper. She was engaged to my father long before Margaret Davenport."

"Was your mother ever married to your father?" asked Mr. Morgan.

Clara frowned. "They were never married, Sir."

"I see. Miss Davenport, I will need to look into my records to learn how to move forward. It may not be today, but I will send you a post when I have an answer for your claim," explained Mr. Morgan.

"You need not send a post. Davenport House has a telephone now. Let me tell you the number."

Mary and Abigail felt a renewed sense of strength as they rode over the fields with Ethan alongside them. The three of them wondered why they had not been riding sooner. They leisurely made their way back to the stable. Throughout the ride, Mary was gathering the courage to speak with John Smith for the first time since reading the letter. Mary explained that she would do so while Ethan put the horses away. She disappeared up the staircase behind the stable to see if John was in the apartment. Abigail and Ethan remained in the stable and found a haystack for a seat. Ethan held Abigail's hand in his, and they smiled at each other, grateful to have this moment alone. They were quiet for a long time until it was clear that Mary would not be returning for a while.

"Has she been alright?" Ethan asked Abigail.

"Mary seems cheerful under the circumstances. Perhaps she has always known in her heart. But Ethan, how do you feel about it?"

He looked down. "I only hope she can be happy with us."

Mary knocked on the door of the apartment where Ethan and his father lived. John was quick to open the door. Mary stood there awkwardly. "I have read the letter," she said quietly. He nodded in response. "If it is not too difficult, would you please—tell me about my real family?" John Smith nodded again and invited Mary into the sitting room.

"Miss Mary, I thought that my mind was playing tricks on me all these years. When you would say a thing or your face looked a certain way, I thought, it is just what my little girl would have looked like if she had lived. Many times it was hard to be around you because I could not stop thinking of her. I guess I never thought—you could have been her all along."

"I am sorry that it is difficult for me to address you as

Father. It is what I am used to calling the man who raised me," said Mary nervously.

"I understand," John assured her. "Don't you worry about that. It will take time for the news to sink in for all of us. The Master was a good man. I am glad to know it was he who raised you as his own, if it couldn't have been me."

"Would you really have killed the doctor, if you had known what he did?"

"Your mother knew me well. I was quicker to act in those days without thinking it through. I got mixed with the wrong people that got me in prison," he answered with a sigh. "She was right to withhold it from me. I fear to think how I would have left my son an orphan, if I had known the truth."

"But the law surely found you innocent if you were released from prison," Mary said.

"That is another story, and it involves a woman who was kinder to me than I deserved. It was your mother's sister, Louisa."

Down in the stable, Abigail continued to talk with Ethan while she waited for Mary. "There must be plenty to say between those two," Abigail remarked. "I wonder if Mary realizes it is nearly time for dinner."

"I should bring the horses in," said Ethan, stifling a yawn. "Pa and I have not slept much since reading that letter."

Abigail stood up from the haystack. "I should be getting back to the house. I will instruct for Mary's dinner to be taken to her room." Mary walked into the stable just then. She looked very tired.

"I am going back to the house now. I think I will go right to sleep. Go ahead and have dinner without me,

Abigail," Mary told her. Ethan looked at Mary lovingly and hugged her goodbye. Mary smiled at him, then left the stable, seemingly in a daze.

Abigail started to follow Mary, but stumbled after a cracking sound was heard. Ethan quickly caught Abigail before she fell. "Are you alright?" he asked her. "What happened?"

"Oh dear, it is my shoe. The heel has finally broken off. I meant to see the cobbler before this happened," she answered.

Ethan still held her and smiled. "I can carry you back to the house," he offered.

Abigail felt her cheeks burning. "I do not want to be any trouble. I am certain that I can walk."

"You are never any trouble, Abigail," he chuckled as he lifted her in his arms. "I don't mind one bit."

Most everyone had retired to bed after dinner. Bridget sat on the bed in Fiona's new room in the servant's quarters. Fiona was marking her checklist with a pen to assure that everything had been done for the day. "Fiona," her sister began. "Do you think we will ever see Mother and Father again?"

Fiona sighed. "I do miss them. I especially miss our sisters. But we are needed here, Bridget. It is because of you and me that our family is able to eat every night. Mother wrote to me just today that she is with child again."

"Oh, I do hope it is a boy this time!" exclaimed Bridget with a smile. "Mother and Father deserve a son, at least."

Fiona giggled, for she and Bridget had seven younger sisters. "If it is a son, he will know everything about women. He won't be able to help it."

Bridget sighed dreamily. "I saw the most wonderful

thing in the world today. Miss Abigail broke the heel of her boot, and the stable boy carried her all the way to the house and up the staircase to her room. Then he smiled at me when he left the room. Isn't he the most handsome man you have ever seen?"

Fiona sighed as well. "I do believe he is. I hope his engagement with Abigail still stands. You are not still worried, are you?"

"No, I am certain that he loves her now. But Fiona, there is something peculiar happening in the house. I do not know what it is, but it seems to involve Mrs. Price."

"I am inclined to agree. Everyone seems to be acting strange. I do hope whatever it is may be resolved quickly so that things may return to normal."

The next morning, Mary had changed into her riding clothes and was leaving her bedroom. Fiona met her on the upstairs landing.

"Did I just hear the telephone ring?" asked Mary hopefully.

"You did, Miss Mary. It is Mr. Morgan from the trustee's office. He wishes to speak with you."

"Father's trustee?" Mary asked in surprise. "I have not seen him in months. I wonder what he could be calling about."

Clara had also heard the telephone ring, and spoke briefly with Mr. Morgan just before Mary arrived to the library. Clara was too nervous to speak to Mary just then, so she quietly hurried away to the drawing room to find Mrs. Price. "Mother, I must speak with you. I would like you to accompany me to town today. There is something that I think you must witness. I hope you understand that I am only trying to help."

"Sounds mysterious," replied Mrs. Price. "I was wondering when you would invite me to ride in your new motor car."

Clara smiled. "You will love it, Mother. It is lightning fast!"

Mary had just hung up the telephone with Mr. Morgan when Abigail walked into the library. "Mary, would it be alright for me to order the car today? I do need to see the cobbler without delay."

Mary looked bewildered. "I have just spoken to father's trustee. He has instructed that I should come to his office, urgently. But Abigail, do you think he could have found out? I am suddenly worried."

"I do not see how it is possible. Mrs. Price has proven that she can hold a secret indefinitely," Abigail remarked.

"I will order the car now and change out of my riding clothes. You can do anything you need in town while I meet with Mr. Morgan."

"Thank you, Mary. I do hope everything will be alright."

Phillip drove Mary and Abigail to Yorktown. Mary went into the trustee's office and Abigail stayed in the car while she looked into her purse. She retrieved the broken heel and held it in her hand.

"What do you have there?" Phillip asked curiously.

Abigail giggled. "It is the heel to my boot. It came off yesterday and I must have it repaired."

"I see. I will assist you to the cobbler's shop," offered Phillip as he helped Abigail out of the car.

Mary informed the secretary at the trustee's office of her arrival. Mary then turned to sit in the small lobby when she observed that Clara and Mrs. Price were waiting there.

Before Mary had a chance to react, the secretary announced to the ladies, "Mr. Morgan will see you now."

"Mary, I know you must be surprised to see me here," Clara said to her quietly as they walked down the hallway. "Just know that whatever happens today, I promise to take care of you, as you have taken care of me."

Mr. Morgan was solemn at his desk while Mrs. Price, Clara, and Mary were seated in chairs across from him. "Miss Davenport," he said, looking at Mary. "I have asked you to come today because of information which has recently come to my attention. I received affidavits from Mrs. Davenport about the circumstances of your birth. Unfortunately, since a formal adoption was never conducted, your inheritance was unlawful. I have been forced to reopen Mr. Davenport's estate."

The color drained from Mary's face. She sat speechless as she tried to understand the words she had been told. Clara looked sorrowfully at Mary, and was beginning to feel sick in her stomach. She soon regretted that she had ever stepped foot into Mr. Morgan's office with those papers.

Mr. Morgan turned to Clara. "On the subject of the claim you presented for yourself just yesterday, Miss Davenport, I am unable to be of service. The state law does not recognize illegitimate children as legal heirs. You have stated that your mother and father were never married. The circumstances of your birth invalidates your claim."

Mrs. Price looked at her daughter in horror. "What have you done, Child?" she asked. "Mr. Morgan, what does this mean? Who is to inherit the estate if not Mr. Davenport's own children?"

Mr. Morgan sighed heavily. "I am afraid that the estate

is now declared property of the state of Pennsylvania. It will be sold at auction."

Just then, a tall woman in a long black dress walked in, ignoring the objections of Mr. Morgan's secretary. "Please wait your turn, Mrs. Davenport. Mr. Morgan is with a client," the secretary pleaded.

Mrs. Davenport continued walking right up to the desk. "I will be quick, Mr. Morgan," she said briskly. "When will the estate be auctioned?" Mary's heart sank into her stomach. She had not seen Mrs. Davenport in several weeks, and the sight of her made Mary feel ill.

"Thirty days from today, Mrs. Davenport," he answered her.

"I will be there," she stated. She turned to look directly at Clara. "Thank you for your help," Mrs. Davenport said with a smirk, then turned on her heel and walked out of the office. The three shocked ladies remained in their seats.

"I am sorry that this was not the news that any of you wished to hear," apologized Mr. Morgan. "James Davenport was a good man. I have looked at the law from every angle I could imagine to spare you this result, but I am restricted by the language of the Will which only allows for legitimate children of natural birth. Sadly, there is nothing further I can do. You may keep your personal wardrobe and jewelry. However, furniture, livestock, bank accounts, and automobiles are assets of the estate and must remain for auction."

"Our horses!" Mary gasped.

"The horses must stay," Mr. Morgan confirmed, nodding sadly at Mary. "I suggest that you speak with the servants so they may have ample time to find new employment. If you have relatives you may live with, now is the time to make arrangements."

Abigail walked away from the cobbler shop wearing her newly repaired boots. She was just about to walk back to the car when she heard a familiar sound that made her heart beat with joy.

"Poundies!" called a boy with a thick Irish accent. "Five cents. Would ya like a portion, Sir?" The boy sat with a basket under the awning of a shop and called to the passersby.

"Get outta here, Irish!" the man called back angrily as he kicked his boot into the dirt near the boy. Abigail hurried over as the man walked away.

"Are you alright, Dear?" she asked the boy.

He hung his head. "I am alright, Miss."

"Poundies are my favorite," she said kindly. "I would like to buy some."

The boy looked up at her. "Ya would, Miss? It is my last portion. Mummy has been sick and cannot work. I have sold poundies so we can buy bread."

Abigail's heart went out to the boy who sat there dressed in rags. He was not wearing shoes and Abigail was sure that he did not have any. She reached into her purse and found two dollar coins. "Give these to your mother, Dear," she said, extending the coins to him.

The boy's face lit up. "Thank ya, Miss!" He then gave Abigail the potatoes wrapped in tin foil and gripped the coins tightly in his hand before running down the street. Abigail giggled in delight. She gazed sentimentally at the whipped potatoes while warm childhood memories filled her heart.

Phillip was waiting near the car when Abigail returned. "Is Mary still with the trustee?" Abigail asked in surprise.

"She has not come out yet," Phillip answered. Abigail stood with him under the awning of a shop to be shielded from the sun.

"I do hope everything is alright," said Abigail in concern. "How are Gabriella and Donnie? And your dear sister?"

Phillip smiled. "The children are well. They have taken a liking to Serena. I do not think they even notice when I am gone, now," he teased.

"I am glad to hear they are doing well. I have been sorry to not visit more often."

"You are welcome anytime you can," Phillip replied sincerely. "Serena has expressed that she would like to see you again."

Abigail giggled. "We barely exchanged any words at all. I am surprised that Serena remembers who I am."

Phillip looked sheepish. "I suppose it is because I speak about you so often."

"You do?" Abigail questioned.

"I—I worry there might have been a misunderstanding before—when I asked you for your hand," he stammered. "You answered that you thought I might only be asking for the little ones. But it was more than that. I wanted to marry you then because you are the kindest woman I've met. I still want to marry you now," he confessed quietly.

Abigail stared at him, her eyes wide with shock. "Phillip, I am going to marry Ethan," she replied frantically.

Phillip was surprised. "Oh! I apologize, Miss Abigail. I did not know!"

"Clara did not tell you?"

"She never said. Forgive me, please. If I had known, I never would have—" Phillip was interrupted by the sight of Mary approaching them from the trustee's office. She looked pale and distressed.

"Mary, what has happened?" asked Abigail.

"We have lost everything," Mary whispered. "The estate will be auctioned and we must find a new home. I cannot face the servants now, Abigail. Please—when we get home—tell them for me."

Clara and Mrs. Price rode home in silence. Clara had never been so ashamed in her life. She felt sick knowing that she had a hand in ruining the lives of everyone she loved and cared for. Clara wondered if she should confront Mrs. Davenport for tricking her about the Will.

Abigail solemnly addressed the staff who had gathered in the Hall of Davenport House. "Something terrible has happened today that will affect all of us most wretchedly. Mary no longer owns the estate and the house and property will be sold at auction. We are given thirty days to make other living and working arrangements. I am very sorry to everyone that this has happened."

The maids looked at each other helplessly, but no one said a word. Bridget began to cry. Mary, Clara, and Mrs. Price hung their heads in sorrow. The front door swung open just then and Mrs. Davenport made a grandiose entrance, walking tall and proud. She clapped her hands together loudly to command everyone's attention. "What a gloomy moment I must have walked in on. Do not despair, for I intend to buy the house at auction. Most of you will still have your jobs," she proclaimed to the staff, then turned to look directly at Mrs. Price. "Others of you will not be so fortunate."

"This is all your doing!" cried Clara angrily. "You said the estate would belong to me. I want my money returned immediately!"

Mrs. Davenport threw back her head and laughed. "You stupid girl. You are not even a person in the eyes of the law. We had a deal, and I have held up my end by providing the documents. Do not worry, Clara. I do not intend to leave you on the streets with your mother. I always thought you performed splendidly as a maid to Mary. You can be maid to me if you wish to stay in the house. Fiona, come take my hat and gloves, and send someone to collect my things. I am moving back into my old room."

Mary and Abigail sat quietly in Mary's room staring blankly in front of them. "I suppose I never deserved this life," said Mary, feeling defeated. "I should have been a servant all along."

"I am terribly sorry, Mary. What will you do?" asked Abigail.

Mary sighed. "I plan to be at dinner tonight. I am curious what Mother has to say about why she gave those documents to the trustee. I am confused about how Clara was involved with her. Did Mother and Clara plan to take the inheritance from me? I do not understand how it happened. Abigail, you are the only one in the house who I can trust now."

Mrs. Price packed her traveling case while Clara whimpered behind her. "Please speak to me, Mother," she begged. "I was only trying to help the estate. Mrs. Davenport tricked me."

Her mother sighed. "I cannot stay here another

moment. I will go to a boarding house until I find new employment. I wish that you would come with me, Clara. But I know you do not like being told what to do."

"I know I often spoke of wanting to get away, but this house is all that I know. For the first time, I am frightened to leave it," admitted Clara.

"It is not so terrible in the outside world. If you have survived Davenport House until now, you should have no trouble adjusting to a new house," Mrs. Price assured her. "You are welcome to come with me or stay here, but remember that the house does not belong to Margaret until she buys it. For now, it belongs to the state. Do not let Margaret bully you. Remember, she is only a Davenport by marriage, but you are a Davenport by blood."

In the city of Yorktown, William was preparing the clinic to be closed for the day, relieved that there were no other cases of typhoid that week. He was about to retire to his apartment upstairs when there was a knock at the door of the clinic. William answered the door to find a man in an expensive suit and polished shoes. The man looked William up and down. "Are you Dr. Hamilton?" he asked, wrinkling his nose in annoyance.

"I am. How may I be of service?" replied William.

"You may stop fraternizing with my fiance," the man replied sternly.

William was taken aback. "Um—there must be a mis-understanding. I only attend to my patients as they need medical care. If your fiance is a patient of mine, then I cannot be expected to neglect my duty."

The man laughed incredulously. "She is no patient. You've been seen at her house, coming and going on several occasions. I have come to tell you to stop. I require her reputation to be intact."

"This has to be a mistake. I do not know who your fiancé is," William answered flustered. "I only make house calls when there is a medical need."

"Then I trust you have no reason to return to Davenport House. Mary Davenport and I are engaged to be married, and we intend to seal our union as soon as she is out of mourning. Good day, Doctor." The man turned to leave the clinic. William was speechless and felt his chest tightening until he could hardly breath. His head was spinning as he clutched the cold handrail of the spiral staircase. He took each heavy step to his apartment above the clinic where he collapsed in his bed, rethinking all that he thought he knew.

Mary and Mrs. Davenport were the only ones in the dining room that night. Mrs. Davenport seemed to be eating heartily, but Mary stared blankly at her own plate, which remained as full as it was when it left the kitchen.

"Honestly, Mary, did you really think that I would poison you?" Mrs. Davenport asked suddenly. "It was I who took you in as an orphan and gave you this grand life. How could you think that I did not care for you?"

Mary could feel her heart sinking into her stomach. She had suspected Mrs. Davenport of attempting to poison her only months ago, but now Mary did not know what to think. Instead of answering the question, Mary asked one of her own. "If you cared for me, then how could you give the trustee those papers that leave me penniless?"

"Oh, do not be sore about that, Mary. You will have it all back eventually. When I am dead," Mrs. Davenport added. "I could not stand idly by and watch the estate be mismanaged into ruin. The first thing you did was give half of it away to that stupid maid. Your spending has been frivolous ever since. You must imagine how difficult it was for me to see all of my years of hard work slowly come apart."

Mary did not know how to argue with that. It was true that she had struggled with the finances ever since she became Mistress of Davenport House. "I was only doing what I thought Father would have wanted," she replied honestly.

"He was never good with these decisions, either. But let us not think back about unpleasant things. I am going to change the subject to something more cheerful. It is time for you to be married. I have already arranged a match for you, and you may plan your wedding as elaborate as you wish."

Mary looked up in disbelief. "You have arranged a match for me? Who?"

"Charles Squire. The Squire family estate is grand indeed. I am certain that you will like the house," Mrs. Davenport stated confidently. "Do not look at me so hopelessly, Mary. Trust me that it is for the best. You and I are not so different, you know. We both may have turned our affections toward the town doctor, but let's face it, a doctor's wages cannot support ladies like us. We must be realistic."

"You still speak of me as if I was your daughter," Mary said in a low voice. "Yet you have taken steps to prove to Mr. Morgan that I am not."

"That is only to Mr. Morgan. As far as society is concerned, I will still treat you as my daughter. You are fortunate. Not many orphans could dream of such a life."

"I cannot imagine marrying a man who I do not even know," Mary stated bluntly.

"You will have to trust me that it is better this way.

Marrying for love might seem romantic at your age, but it can cause you more heartache than marrying a stranger. I hope that you never know the pain of loving a man who does not return your affection."

Mary looked at her skeptically. "Do you mean to say that you truly loved Father?"

"Of course I did," Mrs. Davenport snapped. "How could you question it? You cannot know what I suffered, being forced to live with his former lover, when he never cared for me as much as he did her. I used to be optimistic like you, Mary. Life has hardened me forever to the notion of marrying for love. You will thank me someday for arranging your marriage into the Squire family. It was no easy feat, and I am certain that even your father would be impressed."

Mary wondered how much Mrs. Davenport knew. "But, who are my real parents?"

"Do not bother yourself with unpleasant things, Mary. I suspect that your mother was a working girl who needed to rid herself of a child in order to resume—that way of life. Lord only knows who your father may have been. I doubt that your mother would have been particular in her customers. I did not ask questions when I took you in, and I chose to turn a blind eye to the circumstances of your birth. Let us not worry about the details and we will continue to live as if you have always been a Davenport. You can thank me by entering gracefully into the marriage that I have arranged for you. It will benefit both of our families. No one need ever hear of the kind of woman your mother really was."

Mary was seething as she jumped from her seat. "Do not dare speak about my mother again!" she screamed at the top of her lungs. "I do not want to be your daughter!

Ever!" Mary stormed away, blinded by her tears and rage. Mrs. Davenport calmly ate her meal as if nothing had happened at all.

It was late that night when Mrs. Price arrived at Wilkes' Boarding House in Lancaster. It was run by a widow called Mrs. Wilkes, and had several modest yet comfortable guest rooms. Mrs. Wilkes showed Mrs. Price to a small bedroom in the attic with only the flame of a candle to light the way. Mrs. Price was well prepared for living away from Davenport House. When Margaret Davenport was the Mistress, Mrs. Price always felt that her days as housekeeper were numbered. She saved the bulk of her wages for an occasion such as this. She settled into the room and changed into her nightclothes and bonnet. She then squinted her eyes in the dimly lit room to read the listings on the newspaper she brought with her. A great house in Lancaster was in want of a housekeeper. Mrs. Price planned to respond to the listing the next day.

In the servants' lobby of Davenport House, the maids discussed the new arrangements and changes that would take place with Mrs. Davenport living in the house again. Fiona felt uncomfortable whenever Clara's driver Stuart lurked near the maids. He would speak to them in a familiar way and called each of them "sweetheart". He would also stand very close to them or intentionally brush against them in the hallways. Fiona did not feel like she had the authority to ask him to leave, but she did not want him to bother the maids, either. It was unheard of for a young female servant to have leadership over a male servant, so Fiona kept silent. After the staff meeting, Bridget followed Fiona into her bedroom. "I do not like that new chauffeur," Bridget whispered. "The way he looks at me makes me feel ill."

Fiona sighed. "I feel the same way about him. I have noticed that I feel relieved every time Miss Clara must order the car, for I know it means we will be rid of him for the day. With all of the changes in the house, I do not know if Miss Clara will need him so much anymore. I hope that Mrs. Davenport requires Stuart to drive her often. I do not like him living in the servants' quarters with us while Mrs. Price is gone."

CHAPTER 9

Abigail visited Mary's bedroom the next morning. Mary told Abigail about her exchange with Mrs. Davenport the night before. The two girls opted to have their breakfast upstairs that day. "Mary, I have spoken with Ethan about your mother—um, Mrs. Davenport's—return. Ethan's father has kindly offered to let us move into their apartment with them. Ethan will give up his room for you and I to share."

Mary's eyes grew wide. "But there is not room for all four of us in such a small space," she said in concern.

Abigail giggled. "I have lived in such a space with my family of thirteen. It is possible, Mary. Trust me."

"Where will we put all of our things?" asked Mary.

"Perhaps you may pick out only your favorite clothes to bring. You have not worn most of your dresses since you began mourning."

Mary sighed. "I suppose it is improper for me to be in mourning for my father now, when my true father is alive. It must be bad luck for me to continue wearing black."

"Whatever you decide, I am sure it will be the right

decision. I only wanted to tell you of a chance to live away from the house. I know it is difficult with Mrs. Davenport staying," Abigail offered gently.

Bridget brought in breakfast trays for Mary and Abigail. "Miss Mary," she said. "The Mistress instructed me to tell you that Mr. Charles Squire will be arriving in the afternoon, and that you should be ready to be presented."

"Thank you, Bridget," Mary answered, sounding distressed.

After Bridget left the room, Abigail asked Mary, "Who is Charles Squire?"

Tears were forming in Mary's eyes. "No one important. Come, help me choose which clothes to bring when I move in with my true family."

Mrs. Price was seated at the breakfast table at Wilkes' Boarding House. She felt a familiar sensation when the door to the kitchen was opened and the aroma filled the dining room. Mrs. Price was certain that she recognized the cooking. After breakfast, she excused herself from the table and asked if she might compliment the cook. Mrs. Wilkes was pleased to oblige and allowed Mrs. Price entry into the kitchen.

"Mrs. Malone?" called Mrs. Price as she entered the kitchen.

"Dorothy Price!" cried the former cook of Davenport House. "Good gracious, I never thought I would see anyone from the house again. Have you come to find me?"

"I had no idea that you would be here. I am staying as a guest until I find a new position. I am no longer employed by Davenport House," she answered.

"What has happened?" asked Mrs. Malone. "The last I heard, you had gotten a promotion."

"I had. But the former Mistress has returned and I

cannot stay in the house any longer. She has arranged for Miss Mary to lose every penny of her inheritance!"

Mrs. Malone's face turned red with anger. "How did that dreadful woman get out of jail?"

Mrs. Price was surprised at this reaction. "The evidence against her was apparently insufficient. Mrs. Davenport is now thought to be innocent."

Mrs. Malone yanked off her apron and slammed it down on the butcher block table. "That woman doesn't have an innocent bone in her body! She insisted that she be the one to take the Master his tea the last week I was employed at the house. I don't know what she had going with that doctor, but they put something in the Master's drink. I am sure of it!"

Mrs. Price's eyes grew wide. "Then she did have a hand in poisoning him. Oh, Heavens! I have left my daughter and Miss Mary alone with that dangerous woman! What have I done?" Mrs. Price was frantic and looked as though she would leave for Davenport House that very minute.

"Wait!" cried Mrs. Malone. "Dorothy, before you go—I have something to show you. You might not like that I took it from the Master's library. Just try to understand that I did it to protect Miss Mary. If she has already lost the house, then there is no need for me to conceal it any longer."

Ethan helped Abigail and Mary move their things into his home above the stable. The ceiling was sharply slanted on one side of the small room. "I'm sorry it is not what you're used to, Miss Mary," Ethan said quietly.

Mary looked at him endearingly. "I do not think there is any need for you to address me that way anymore. I am your sister, and I am grateful to you for giving up your room for us."

Ethan smiled sympathetically in response, then left the room so that Abigail and Mary could settle in. After he left the room, Mary whispered, "There is only one bed. I do not know how we will manage!"

Abigail giggled at her. "I once shared a bed this size with six of my siblings."

Mary looked aghast. "How?"

"Well, three would lie here," Abigail said as she pointed to the bed. "The other three would lie here, and I was in the middle. The trick was to lie very still and try not to fall off the bed."

"I cannot tell if you are teasing me!" Mary exclaimed.

Abigail laughed. "It is the honest truth, Mary. Many people live like this, you know. The families who have grand houses like yours are the exception."

Mary felt embarrassed. "I suppose I never thought of it. Please be patient with me while I do my best to adjust. It is a very different life for certain."

"Of course, Mary," Abigail replied. "Ethan said that he will cook for us tonight. You and I can make tomorrow's dinner."

Mary's eyes grew wide. "Then you will have to be patient with me in the kitchen as well. I have never been in one before." She sighed. "There is one thing I must do before I leave my house for good. In the past, I have encouraged William to visit as often as he could. I cannot receive him at the house now."

Mary walked carefully into the grand library, looking around to make sure that no one saw her. She hoped that she would not run into Mrs. Davenport that day. She only wanted to telephone William before she began her new life above the stable. When William answered the phone, Mary suddenly felt awkward about what she had to say. "William? I have telephoned you to inform you that…my circumstances have changed," she said hesitantly. She could hear William sigh into the phone.

"I know, Mary," he replied.

"You do?" she asked in surprise. Mary was astonished and dismayed that word had already reached William about her lost inheritance.

"Yes—and I wish you the best," he answered. It sounded as though the words pained him to speak.

"I am afraid that I cannot receive you at the house anymore, but I will still come to town to visit you," she assured him.

"I am sorry, but I must be off the telephone now. It appears there has been another outbreak and new patients have just arrived. I wish you joy in your new life, and please be careful about coming into town. Goodbye, Mary."

Mary could feel her heart sinking as she slowly replaced the receiver. William's voice sounded as though he could not wait to be off the telephone with her. Mary suddenly realized that she must not be desirable anymore, now that she was poor and living like a servant. She sorrowfully left the library and walked away from the house, thinking that it would be for the last time.

Mrs. Squire and her son Charles arrived to Davenport House that afternoon as expected. Mrs. Davenport greeted them warmly in the Hall, then proceeded to take them on a tour throughout the house. Fiona set out tea in the drawing room after the tour. She stood by with Bridget as Mrs. Davenport, Charles Squire, and Mrs. Squire, were seated in the drawing room.

"There are one thousand acres total, with lovely woodlands and fields," Mrs. Davenport was saying. "I assume that your son has found the library to his satisfaction. There are many rare and expensive books within the shelves."

Charles Squire nodded then looked at his mother. "And where is the girl?" asked Mrs. Squire, seemingly bored.

Mrs. Davenport smiled. "Bridget, please summon Mary to the drawing room. Mrs. Squire, she is no longer a girl, but has blossomed into a beautiful woman since you saw her last. I am sure that Mary will meet with your enthusiastic approval."

Bridget returned to the drawing room without Mary. "Forgive me, Madam, but I cannot find Miss Mary," she reported nervously.

Mrs. Squire raised her eyebrow at Mrs. Davenport. "Remember our bargain, Margaret. If your daughter is not agreeable to this arrangement, we will not help you with the funds."

"Oh, I am afraid there was only a miscommunication in our schedules today," Mrs. Davenport said with a smile. "My daughter is honored to become part of your family."

After the Squires left the house, Bridget whispered to Fiona on their way to the servants' stairs. "I do not understand. The Mistress expressed that she intends to buy the house when it goes to auction. But when the Squires were here, she showed them the house as if she intends to sell it to them."

Fiona sighed heavily. "I do not think it is the house that

the Mistress intends to sell," she replied. "Mrs. Davenport appears to be trading her daughter in marriage for the means to buy the house now, with the understanding that it will eventually belong to the Squires. I have heard that important families make these arrangements with their children."

"But Miss Mary loves Dr. Hamilton!" Bridget protested. "I cannot believe that she will agree to this."

"Perhaps it is why she was absent today," Fiona replied. "None of us can be certain of what the future holds for us now."

Mary and Abigail were settled into their new home. "Something is bothering me, Abigail. I telephoned William, and he has said that there is another fever outbreak in town. We should stay away for the time being. Somehow, William has already heard that I have lost the house. He said that he wished me well, but I had the feeling that he was uncomfortable speaking to me."

"It is difficult to tell what a person is feeling when you cannot observe them in person," reminded Abigail. "Perhaps he was only worried about the outbreak, and that is why you detected discomfort in his voice."

Mary thought for a moment. "I hope that was it. But I cannot let go of the feeling that it was something else."

"Ethan tells me that dinner will soon be ready," Abigail said to Mary, hoping to take her mind off worries about William.

"Oh, thank you," Mary said, looking up from the book she was holding. "What will you wear to dinner tonight?"

"I had not planned to change. I will wear what I am wearing now," answered Abigail. "Our dinners here will not be the formal ones you are used to."

Mary smiled. "Perhaps it is a relief that I need not dress differently for dinner. It does get tiring changing clothes all day long."

Mary and Abigail sat at the small table with Ethan and John Smith. Each had a bowl of stew in front of them. Mary could find carrots and potatoes in the broth, but wondered if Ethan had forgotten to add the meat. She did not want to mention it and appear ungrateful. It was a different life than she was raised in, but the feeling of tranquility that settled upon the dining area was a feeling that she was glad to become used to.

Back at Davenport House, Clara was gazing sorrowfully at the black uniform she used to wear when she worked as a maid. Her future suddenly seemed grimmer than it ever had in the past. She was sure that Mary must hate her, and Clara could not blame her for it. She wished that she could tell Mary how sorry she was, but she could not find her in the house all day, and was worried she would run into Mrs. Davenport if she looked further. Clara looked at her reflection in the vanity mirror, wondering what she had become. Her thoughts were interrupted by a knock at her bedroom door.

"Mother!" Clara exclaimed in surprise. She was overcome with emotion and threw her arms around her mother.

"I am here, Child. Everything is going to be alright," Mrs. Price consoled her. She still wore her hat and carried her traveling case as if she had just come through the front door.

"I regretted that I did not go with you, Mother. I feel like a prisoner here," Clara cried. "Please tell me that you have come to take me away from this house."

"I have not come to take you away. I have come to tell you that from this day forward, Davenport House belongs to you, and no one else."

Clara looked skeptically at her mother. "I don't understand. Has the trustee found a way for me to inherit?"

"Your father found a way for you to inherit," Mrs. Price replied, handing Clara a document. "This is a petition to the Court of the Common Plea. Your father asked the court for permission to adopt you before he died. You had been made a legitimate child and heiress, only we did not know it," Mrs. Price explained with tears in her eyes.

Clara gasped. "Where did you find this?"

"It is a long story, Child. But there is more. The Will of your father's that was never found—Mrs. Malone has kept it with her all this while."

"Why would she do such a thing?" asked Clara.

"Your father left you everything, Clara. Mrs. Malone believed that she protected Miss Mary by keeping the Master's intentions hidden. I have seen the Will, and I left it with the trustee today. I also showed him this petition to the court. Mr. Morgan has confirmed it for his records. You never need worry about your place in this house again."

Clara sat down on her bed in disbelief. "But Mother, this is dreadful. What about Mary? She will be devastated to hear this. She loved Father so dearly and will be hurt that he did not recognize her."

"That is why Mrs. Malone kept the documents. She was afraid that Miss Mary would not receive her rightful inheritance. I am at a loss to explain it myself, especially after the Master told me that he would leave all to her. I do not know what changed his mind, but it is clear now that this is what your father wished. He must have had his reasons."

Clara sighed. "I still feel for Mary. I wish that I could rejoice at this news you have given me tonight, but I do not know how I can be happy when Mary has lost everything. She was good to me when I never deserved it."

Mrs. Price felt a wave of emotions wash over her and placed her hand over her heart. "Never have I been so proud of you as I am in this moment, Child. I know you will do what is right. Now…there is something further that I must do. Goodnight, Clara."

Mrs. Price then went to the door of Mrs. Davenport's bedroom. She swung the door open without knocking. "What is the meaning of this?" cried Mrs. Davenport from her bed. "Why have you returned? I will have you thrown out!"

"It is too late for your threats now, Margaret. The Master's Will and petition to adopt Clara have reached the trustee. Everything now belongs to my daughter—and you are trespassing," Mrs. Price said sternly.

"You are lying. No one could possibly have found his Will," Mrs. Davenport sneered. "I searched the house from top to bottom and never found a thing."

"It is because Mrs. Malone has had it in her possession all this while. She was displeased to hear that you have been released from jail, and has gone to the police with further testimony against you."

The color drained from Mrs. Davenport's face. "What has she said? It is only lies, I am sure."

"That will be for the judge to decide. For now, I suggest that you run. You may not get far before you are made to pay for your crimes, but do not think that you will hide in my daughter's house another moment."

Mrs. Davenport began to pack her things into a traveling case. Mrs. Price left the room, feeling as though the heavy weight she carried for twenty-five years had vanished from her shoulders once and for all.

CHAPTER 10

Before breakfast the next morning, Clara went to the stable. "Ethan?" she called. She could see that he was opening the stalls to take the horses out to the pasture. "Clara? What is it?" he asked.

"We cannot find Mary or Abigail. I wondered if you knew where they might be," Clara answered worriedly.

"Oh," he nodded. "They have moved in with me and Pa. They could not be around the Mistress any longer."

"I see," said Clara. "I really must speak with them. Are they in the apartment now?"

Ethan nodded in response. Clara went up the stairs behind the stable. She took a deep breath and knocked on the door. Mary answered the door and was surprised to see Clara there.

"Mary, I know what you must think of me," began Clara. "I am terribly sorry for the trouble I have caused. I hope that someday you can forgive me. Have you truly left the house to live in this apartment?"

Mary nodded. "I could not stay in the house any longer. Mother tried to force me into a marriage."

"I did not realize, Mary. I can assure you that Mrs. Davenport will not bother you at the house any longer. She has left the house for good."

Mary raised her eyebrows in surprise. "How did you manage that?"

Clara was nervous as she continued. "Something has happened. The last Will that Father wrote has been found." Clara looked at the floor. "He left everything to me. We discovered a document that proved he did adopt me through the court."

Mary tried to hide her disappointment. "I—am happy for you, Clara."

"Come back to the house, Mary. I want it to be your home as much as it is mine. Please, come live with me as my sister again. Abigail is welcome too, of course," Clara offered sincerely.

Mary sighed. "Thank you, Clara. I will tell Abigail. I have much to tell you about…my family."

Clara looked hopeful. "Does this mean you will come back to the house?"

Mary nodded. "I would be honored," she replied. In the back of her mind, she could not understand why the man who she was raised to call Father would not have adopted her as well.

Mary and Abigail moved back into the house, and everyone hoped for a sense of normalcy to someday settle upon it. Mary felt awkward knowing that she was no longer in a position to give orders, and she became aware that her position in the house was at the mercy of Clara. It was a difficult adjustment the first several days, but Mary soon felt relief in knowing that the responsibility of the estate was no longer on her shoulders. Clara had kindly arranged for Mary to receive an income from the estate, as well as ownership of her favorite horse Dolly and the automobile that Mary had purchased. A sense of peace was felt over the house now that Mrs. Davenport had not been seen or heard from.

Clara and Mrs. Price began preparing for a trip to New York. Clara wanted to see the shops and watch a Broadway play before Abigail's wedding to Ethan, which was planned for Saturday. Abigail intended to have a small ceremony in the gardens, then move into the apartment with Ethan and his father after the wedding. The house was buzzing with excitement in anticipation of the eventful week.

Abigail visited Ethan in the stable early in the morning. "Are you ready for Saturday?" she asked with a smile.

Ethan smiled back at her. "I can't wait," he answered. Abigail giggled as Ethan put his arms around her and lifted her up.

"Perhaps I should not leave you two in here without a chaperon," Clara teased as she walked into the stable.

Abigail laughed while Ethan set her back down. "Are you leaving now, Clara?" she asked, observing that Clara was wearing traveling clothes and a hat.

"Yes, we are just going now. Mother is already in the car," Clara answered cheerfully. "I wanted to see you together so that I may give you a wedding present early. I wish to give Amethyst and Silver to the both of you. I know you care for them dearly."

Abigail gasped. "Clara, how wonderful!" she exclaimed, then went to embrace Clara. "What a lovely gesture. I never dreamed that I might have a horse of my own someday!"

Clara was beaming. "It is my pleasure. I must hurry to the car now."

"I wish you a marvelous time in New York," Abigail said sincerely. Clara left Abigail and Ethan in the stable, each smiling brightly.

Ethan patted Silver on the back. "That was generous of her," he remarked. "I was not expecting that at all."

"Clara has become a lovely lady. She is kind to me at the house and sees to it that I am paid an allowance, just as before," said Abigail. "Oh Ethan, it brings me such happiness to know we will be married soon. It seems that it is truly happening, now that we have received our first wedding present."

"Of course it is truly happening," Ethan replied with a smile. "It is all I can think about my whole day."

At the breakfast table, Abigail told Mary the news of her wedding present from Clara. Mary was pleased to hear of Clara's generosity and kindness toward Abigail. The girls later changed into their riding clothes to take Dolly and Amethyst over the trails of the estate.

Clara and her mother arrived in New York where they checked into a suite at The Grand Hotel. The bellhop carried the ladies' cases to the luxurious room. A large vase of flowers greeted them as they entered the doorway, and the fragrance of fresh roses filled the room. "So this is what a hotel is like!" exclaimed Clara. "Isn't it fabulous? I am going to look through the window."

Mrs. Price enjoyed watching her daughter take in the delights of the big city. Mrs. Price was becoming quite taken with them herself. Clara peered through the window overlooking the street. "I never dreamed that so many automobiles would be on the road. We hardly saw any carriages once we arrived in New York. I expect everyone must have their own automobile now."

"They are more affordable than ever before," Mrs. Price remarked. "It used to be that only the upper class could afford the cars."

"Mother, are we at war?" Clara asked abruptly.

Mrs. Price sighed. "Not yet, Child. Why do you ask?"

"When we were in the hotel lobby, I heard some men speak of us being at war."

"It is a source of contention for certain. The Secretary of State has just resigned his post because of it. He was under heavy pressure to support our involvement in the War, but he is a pacifist."

"What is a pacifist?" Clara asked curiously.

"It is a person who does not believe in war," her mother explained.

"Are we pacifists?"

"I have not decided. It seems necessary to avoid war at all costs in some circumstances, but necessary to fight in others. If we are going to join the War, it would mean that young men like Ethan and Mr. Valenti could die young, fighting for a cause they might never have believed in," Mrs. Price replied.

"Oh, I hope they are not called to fight. It would be a terrible loss if something were to happen to Ethan or Phillip."

Mrs. Price paused for a moment. "Clara, why have you decided against Phillip?" she asked carefully.

Clara sighed in disappointment. "It is for a reason that even you would understand, Mother. He is Catholic and wanted me to agree to raise our children that way."

"Heavens," Mrs. Price responded. "What a pity. He seemed to be a good man. You are still attractive, Child. I am certain that you will find a suitable husband in no time. I always wondered what you were thinking when you were with that stable boy."

Clara gasped. "You knew about that?"

Mrs. Price raised her eyebrow. "You cannot imagine that I could miss such a thing. A housekeeper must know the maids' whereabouts at all times. I saw everything that happened in the house. Well, almost everything. I was deceived by Margaret more than once..." she trailed off.

"How could you bear to serve her, after everything she had done to us?" Clara questioned.

"I did what I had to do. I could not have been hired elsewhere in my condition. I suppose I always hoped that once your father saw your face, he would realize his mistake and recognize you as his daughter. Margaret saw to it that you stayed out of his sight. She could see the resemblance, I am certain."

"What made Father finally realize the truth? I don't see why it would have taken him twenty-five years," asked Clara.

Mrs. Price appeared perplexed. "It was mere weeks before his death. He approached me rather suddenly one day to declare his error. He apologized for being wrong about you all those years. I still wonder what happened that must have convinced him that Margaret was never to be trusted."

At Davenport House, Fiona watched from a window as a motor car pulled up in the front drive. A woman who wore a long black dress and black veil stepped out of the car and walked to the door. Fiona could feel her heart pounding in her chest in fear that it was the former Mistress. But when Fiona answered the door, she could tell in an instant that this woman was not Mrs. Davenport. She was meek and soft spoken. She greeted Fiona nervously. "Good afternoon. I have come to see Mr. Davenport, if you please."

Fiona was speechless for a moment. She never had a visitor inquire after the late Mr. Davenport until now. She hung her head in sorrow. "I am sorry, Madam, but the Master is no longer with us."

"When did this happen?" the woman asked in a hoarse whisper.

"In April of this year, Madam."

The woman was silent for a moment, then asked, "Does a man called John Smith still work on the estate?"

"John Smith is the groundskeeper. He lives above the stable, Madam. I will send for him," Fiona offered.

"You need not trouble yourself. I will find him," the woman responded quickly. She walked to the stable and gasped when she saw Ethan there. "John?" she asked uncertainly.

Ethan was perplexed to see the woman. When he first watched her approach in mourning attire, he was worried that Mrs. Davenport had returned. He soon realized that this lady could not be Mrs. Davenport, but there was something familiar about her that Ethan could not understand. "I am Ethan. You must be looking for my pa," he answered her gently.

"The housekeeper told me that John Smith lives here," the woman told him.

"He just went upstairs. I will show you the way, Madam," Ethan offered, and he led the woman up the staircase. He opened the door and told his father that a visitor was asking for him. John came to the door.

"How may I help, Madam?" he greeted.

"John?" the woman asked.

"Louisa," he responded, his voice catching in his throat. He stepped forward and gestured for her to enter the sitting room. His heart felt a familiar sinking at the way Louisa flinched when John extended his arm.

"Please, come into the sitting room," he offered softly. Louisa nodded and seated herself in a chair. John left the door open to allow light into the dark little room. Ethan thought it better to excuse himself so that his father could speak with the visitor alone.

"I did not know that you had a son," Louisa said to John. "He is very handsome. For a moment, I thought that I was looking at you twenty years ago."

"Maryanne never told you of our son? I watched her write you letters all the time," John said in surprise.

"I am afraid that only one of her letters ever reached me. It was when she wrote to tell me of her employment at this house. Father instructed for the servants to burn any correspondence from Maryanne as soon as it arrived. We would never have known of her passing, if not for the notice in the newspaper," Louisa explained sorrowfully.

"Have you lived with your father all this while?" John asked. Louisa nodded in response. John shook his head. "I hoped that you would have been married long ago, and gotten away from that man. If I thought you were still there—"

"It is in the past now," Louisa interrupted him. "Father is dead. It is why I have come here."

"You have come to see me?"

"I—I came to see Mr. Davenport. I did not know that you would still be here. But the housekeeper has told me that Mr. Davenport passed away in April. What happened, John?" Louisa asked anxiously.

John sighed. "It is a complicated matter. He was killed by his own son. The Master discovered that he had been deceived, and he changed his Will to recognize another heir. The way I understand it, the son was afraid to lose his inheritance and got to the Master before anything could change."

"Oh John, I am worried that this may have been my fault! Earlier this year when my father was dying, I wrote a letter to Mr. Davenport. I explained to him that his daughter Mary was truly the daughter of my sister. He wrote back to inform me that his wife had deceived him about the child, and that he would make the appropriate arrangements for his heirs. I never dreamed that it would end like this, or I would never have written."

John Smith was quiet. The sequence of events was beginning to make sense for the first time. "Why did you write to him?"

"It is because I have never married and—I have no heirs. I wished to find Mary and make her heiress to the manor house. It is what I told Mr. Davenport. I was unaware that you also had a son," Louisa explained.

"Miss Mary will appreciate this news," John replied. "We can talk about it later. For now, I am afraid that my sitting room is dimly lit and your veil prevents me from seeing your face. I can find somewhere to place your hat and veil, if you wish."

Louisa looked down. "I suppose I prefer it this way," she said quietly. "I do not look the same as I once did."

John tried to swallow the lump in his throat. "I still want to see you. Please…it has been so long. I know that I must look different too."

Louisa reluctantly lifted the veil over the back of her hair. Her eyes were full of sorrow as she looked back at John. The fair, delicate skin of her face revealed the scars of a life lived under fear and mistreatment. John gazed at her in amazement, looking beyond the pain, past the scars, and seeing only a young face that radiated kindness and love. Louisa reached up to return the veil over her face.

"Wait," John said quickly. "Forgive me for staring— it has been years. You are a good soul, Louisa. You need not hide your face from me. You may not know it, but you are beautiful."

"I do not deserve your attention," Louisa replied, shaking her head. "I am not as good as you might think I am."

"Of course you are," he contradicted.

"I wrote to Mr. Davenport when my father became ill. We thought that it was Father's time to die. But then…he recovered. He became worse than he ever was before. Just days ago, he had me by my wrists when I stood at the top of the staircase," Louisa recounted, carefully running her hand along her arm as she spoke. John could see the marks when her sleeve pulled back. "I thought that he would push me. His eyes said that he would. So I—I pushed him," she said, beginning to weep. "I am a murderer."

John pulled his chair alongside hers and carefully put his arm around her. "You are no murderer, Louisa. You protected yourself and there is no crime in that. I wished that I could have ended him all these years because of how he hurt my wife. If that makes me a murderer in my heart, then so be it. A man who hurts a woman is no man at all." Louisa continued to cry. John was relieved to feel her relax into his arm, and he soon held her carefully while the two of them wept together. The work that John had to do for the day could wait. Nothing was more important than this moment, when two anguished souls could feel the releasing of pain and healing of their hearts.

"I am sorry that I pulled away before, when you were only motioning for me to come into the house," Louisa apologized, sniffling into his shoulder. "I know that you would never hurt me."

"No, I would never hurt you. If you want me to let go of you now, you can tell me. It won't bother my feelings one bit if you say so," John told her quietly.

"It is the first time in my life that I have felt safe. Please, do not let me go."

Abigail and Mary returned from their ride. Ethan told them of his father's visitor, who was still upstairs.

"Oh my, I wonder why she has come today," Mary thought aloud. "I will go inside to change. I should be presentable if I am to meet my mother's sister for the first time. Ethan, please invite them to come to the drawing room of the house when they have finished speaking." Ethan nodded in response, and Mary and Abigail returned to the house.

Louisa and John waited in the drawing room for Mary to come down. "I am nervous," Louisa whispered.

John gently squeezed her hand. "She is kind...like her mother," he said to Louisa. "Miss Mary will be glad to see you."

When Mary entered the room, she was wearing an elegant blue afternoon dress. It was the first time that she wore colors since Mr. Davenport had passed away. "You must be my Aunt Louisa," she greeted cheerfully.

Louisa gasped when she first saw Mary. "John," Louisa whispered. "She looks just like her!"

Mary smiled as she approached Louisa and kissed her on the cheek. "You look like my mother as well. I am glad you have come today. Please allow me to introduce my friend Abigail. She is to be married to my brother Ethan on Saturday."

"I am pleased to make your acquaintance, Abigail," Louisa greeted. She then explained her correspondence with Mr. Davenport. "Mary, he wrote to me that he would not feel right adopting you when your true father still lived. I promised Mr. Davenport that you would be heiress to my estate, and it was only then that he thought to exclude you from his Will. He cared for you dearly and planned to explain to you when the time was right. I am sorry that the time never came."

Mary felt a sense of relief, now that her father's reasons were explained so clearly. "Thank you for telling me these things," she said to Louisa.

"I would like very much for all of you to accompany me back to the manor house," Louisa told everyone in the room. "I intend to transfer it to Mary and Ethan as soon as possible."

Mary could not believe her good fortune. "How generous you are, Aunt Louisa. But, you do not wish to have the house for yourself?"

Louisa shook her head. "I no longer want to live there.

I have thought about moving West and starting a new life for myself. The manor house is lovely though, and I wish it to go to family."

Ethan smiled at Abigail. Perhaps he would have a proper house to provide her with after all. "I would like to see it right away," Ethan stated. Abigail smiled back at him. Plans were made to leave with Louisa to view the manor house that very day.

As everyone prepared to leave in Louisa's motor car, Abigail spoke to Ethan privately. "I am sorry, but I do not think I can go with you today," she said. "I have started to feel ill and I am worried that riding in the car will make it worse."

Ethan looked at her in concern. "Are you alright? I will stay with you if you are unwell."

"Please, go without me," she insisted. "I do not wish to spoil your fun. This will be an important trip for your family to be together. I will lie down and rest."

"Are you certain?" he asked again.

Abigail nodded. "Perhaps it is just too much excitement for one week. Bridget is a dear girl and is very attentive to me. With her to assist me, I will likely be well in the morning."

Ethan leaned forward to kiss her lightly on the cheek and could feel how warm her face was against his. He struggled with whether he should stay or go. He knew that the others were waiting for him in front of the house. He looked into her eyes apologetically. "Goodbye, Abigail. I will see you tomorrow."

Ethan left through the front door and explained to the others that he had one further matter to attend to before he could go. He ran to the Valentis' farmhouse and knocked on the door. Phillip answered, amazed to see Ethan.

"Ethan, good afternoon," greeted Phillip. "How are things at the house?"

"Pa and I are leaving for the day with Mary. It doesn't feel right to leave Abigail and the maids alone without a capable man around. Would you keep an eye on the house when we are gone? In case they need anything."

Phillip nodded. "Of course I'll look after them," he answered. "Safe travels, Ethan."

"Thank you," Ethan replied as he shook hands with Phillip. He ran back to the car and was soon on his way to Philadelphia with the others.

Abigail explained to Bridget that she would not be eating dinner that night. She did not know where these sudden aches and feelings of fatigue had come from. She lay upon her bed and was soon asleep.

Fiona answered the door when Phillip Valenti came to call. "Good evening, Miss," he greeted. "I have come to say that if you ladies need anything, I am just a walk to the south."

Fiona could feel herself blushing when Phillip referred to her as a lady. "Thank you, Mr. Valenti," she responded. Phillip walked back to his farmhouse and Fiona went downstairs to her bedroom to put her feet up. It was not often that she had a day off at Davenport House, and she was determined to get some rest now that the family was away.

Louisa Montgomery arrived at the manor house with John, Mary, and Ethan. Mary was impressed to find that the manor house was even grander than Davenport House. She wondered how a single woman could manage such a monstrosity. After they climbed out of the car, Ethan headed in the direction of the stable. Louisa looked confused. "Doesn't he wish to see the house?" she asked the others.

Mary and John Smith laughed. "He might eventually," answered Mary. "He prefers a simpler way of life."

Louisa smiled. "There is a delightful cottage on the estate that he may enjoy with his new bride. It does not require as much maintenance as the big house."

John took a deep breath before he walked into the gardens alone. He remembered each row of hedges and flowering tree. The memories came rushing back to him as he thought of Maryanne crying on this bench where she often went to escape her father. John could feel tears forming in his eyes while he recalled his life on this property all those years ago. He was not sure that he could be on the estate without experiencing the pain he felt now.

Ethan returned from the stable with a smile on his face. "It will do nicely, Aunt. Thank you," he said.

"Let us go into the house now," Louisa said to the others. "There are fifty rooms and much else to see."

"Aunt Louisa," said Mary. "May we see my mother's bedroom first?"

"Yes, of course," Louisa replied. "It has not changed since—the day she left." They walked into the imposing entryway of the house. Mary admired the marble finishes and lavish chandeliers. Louisa was about to lead them up the grand wooden staircase, but she paused to clutch the rail and began to shake in fear. "It is just up here," she told the others, attempting to keep her composure. John came alongside Louisa and steadied her so that she could walk up the stairs.

"It's alright," he whispered. "Lean on me if you need."

When Mary entered her mother's bedroom, she was overcome with emotion. Fine lace curtains hung from the windows. Tapestries lined the gold-trimmed walls, and the table was set with a freshly polished silver tea set. It was clear that the room had been cared for even while no one lived in it. Mary tried to hold back her tears, but it was no use when she felt Ethan standing next to her, holding her hand in his. The room had a feeling of peace along with sadness. Mary instantly knew that if she could choose any room in the house to be hers, this would be the one.

CHAPTER 11

Bridget went to attend to Abigail the next morning, but found her feverish and unresponsive. Bridget then searched for her sister in the servants' quarters. "Fiona, Miss Abigail will not wake! I think she has a fever," Bridget explained.

"Oh dear," replied Fiona. "Let us see to it that Miss Abigail has fresh tea in her room throughout the day."

Bridget nodded. "I will stay with her." She sat in a chair in Abigail's room, waiting for her to wake. Hours had passed and Abigail appeared to be in a distressed sleep, still unable to wake. Bridget and Fiona became increasingly concerned when Abigail had not improved by the evening. "Should we call the doctor?" Bridget asked.

"I do not know," Fiona answered worriedly. "I have only answered the telephone before, but I am unsure how to call out."

"Is there anyone in the house who would know?" Bridget asked.

"I am afraid not. I will go to the neighbor's house.

Mr. Valenti said he would help us if we needed," answered Fiona. She hurried to the Valentis' farmhouse.

"Fiona, what is it?" Phillip asked in concern when he saw her approach.

"It is Miss Abigail, Sir," Fiona replied breathlessly. "She is unwell and we do not know how to call the doctor. Can you use a telephone?"

Phillip sighed. "I'm sorry, Fiona. I am not familiar with how it works. How bad is she?"

"She has been asleep since yesterday afternoon and she has a terrible fever," Fiona answered.

"I will go to town for the doctor," Phillip promised. He ran to the car and sped away down the drive. Fiona returned to the house to tell Bridget.

Clara and Mrs. Price returned to the house around dinner time. Fiona told them of Abigail's condition and that Phillip had gone for the doctor. "Oh, poor Abigail," Clara said worriedly. She went to Abigail's room where Bridget had been waiting all day.

Clara sat on the bed. "Abigail, Dear," she said, placing her hand to Abigail's forehead. "She is burning up. Let us remove the quilt to see if it helps." Bridget helped her to lift the quilt and Abigail still would not respond.

"Bridget, you look tired. I will stay with her now. You should go rest," Clara suggested kindly.

"Thank you, Miss Clara. I hope Miss Abigail is soon recovered," Bridget replied. She left the room to return to the servants' quarters. Stuart was there talking to Fiona and leaning over her. It did not look like Fiona wanted to speak with him. "Fiona, will you assist me?" Bridget called loudly.

"Of course," Fiona answered, relieved to have a reason

to get away from Stuart. "What is it?" she asked when she and Bridget were alone.

"I was worried for you when I saw Stuart standing so close," Bridget replied.

Fiona grimaced in disgust. "He keeps trying to touch my hair. I despise it when he is near, but I do not know if it is my place to tell Miss Clara. It is proper for me to do so?"

"I do not know," Bridget answered. "What if we ask Mrs. Price to return to the servants' quarters?"

Fiona sighed. "I hate to ask, now that she has been living upstairs. She cannot want to leave now."

"I am worried for Miss Abigail," Bridget said, tears forming in her eyes.

"I am worried too, Bridget," Fiona told her, putting her arms around her sister. "Will you sleep in my bed with me tonight? That way, neither of us has to be alone."

"I will get my things," answered Bridget. She settled into Fiona's new room while Fiona checked several times to be sure that the bedroom door was locked. Fiona climbed into the bed, but could not shake the uneasy feeling that filled the pit of her stomach. She was reaching her hand to turn off the lamp near the bed when the hair on her neck suddenly stood on end, and she heard the sound of the doorknob turning behind her. Bridget gasped and looked at her sister, then at the doorknob which began rattling back and forth.

"It is Stuart! I know it!" Fiona cried in a whisper. She jumped from the bed and propped the back of a chair securely under the doorknob. The door began to shake hard and Fiona backed up to the bed in fear.

"What will we do?" whispered Bridget, her eyes wide with fright.

"I do not know!" cried Fiona. The sisters sat on the bed, holding each other tightly.

Clara was with Mrs. Price in Abigail's room. "I am worried, Mother," Clara said. "What if she doesn't wake up?"

"I don't know, Child. Phillip has gone for the doctor and should return at any moment. Stay here and keep watch. I have just had the most terrible feeling. I do not know why, but I think that I should check on the maids. I will bring more tea when I return," Mrs. Price said, then hurried out of the room.

Bridget and Fiona clung to each other on the bed, watching the door frame bend and creak from the force behind it. The window of the room was too small for the girls to climb out of, although they kept glancing toward the window, hoping it had somehow grown bigger for them to escape. It was not long before the door frame snapped, and Stuart could be seen struggling to push the door against the leaning chair. He was sweaty and breathing hard while he stared at the girls, his black eyes full of evil intent. "Open this door now!" he ordered through his teeth.

Bridget screamed from the bed. Fiona hurried to the desk in the room. The sound of the door shaking and cracking nearly made her faint. She took a letter opener from the desk drawer and gripped it tightly in her hand. She turned to face the shaking door as the chair was about to break in two. Fiona charged Stuart with the blade of the letter opener as the chair fell over and slid across the floor. Stuart seemed to shrink back when he observed the fierceness in her eyes. Fiona continued to approach him while he backed away. Stuart began to retreat into the hallway just as a strong fist appeared from the side and forcefully met with Stuart's jaw. The blow knocked Stuart off his feet and he fell on his back, unconscious in the hallway. Fiona stared in amazement as Phillip Valenti appeared in the doorway.

"Are you ladies alright?" he asked quickly. The sisters nodded gratefully in response. "This man won't be bothering you anymore," Phillip assured them. He roughly lifted Stuart's limp body by the trouser waistband and carried him out the door of the servants' quarters. Mrs. Price arrived just in time to witness Phillip knocking Stuart off his feet and removing him from the hallway. Mrs. Price then found Bridget and Fiona on the bed and inquired after their well being. Fiona explained to her what had happened. When Phillip returned to the servants' quarters, he observed that Mrs. Price was waiting for him there. "I am sorry you had to see that, Ma'am," he apologized to her.

Mrs. Price managed a smile. "No need to apologize, Mr. Valenti. I am afraid that I misjudged you. The house is grateful to you for your service," she replied humbly.

"I am sorry to report that I could not bring Dr. Hamilton back with me. He is busy at the clinic and waits for doctors to arrive from Philadelphia to assist in the outbreak. Dr. Hamilton said that he will come as soon as he is able. He was distressed to hear about Miss Abigail," Phillip explained.

"We must make do until he arrives," answered Mrs. Price.

Mary, Ethan, and John arrived at Davenport House late that night with Louisa. They had all expected to return earlier in the day, but soon discovered that none of them wanted to part from each other at the manor house. It was the first time that Mary felt like a true family with her father and brother, and now with an aunt she adored. Mary quickly grew attached to Louisa and hardly paid attention to the manor house anymore, instead savoring each moment that she heard new things about what her mother was like. Not wanting their short time together to be over just yet, Mary invited her aunt to return with them to Davenport House for one more day.

As soon as they walked into the house, Mary could tell that something was wrong. She had a sinking feeling in her stomach as she watched Clara descend the grand staircase to meet them. Clara's expression was grim and she quickly informed them of Abigail's fever, which seemed to grow worse by the minute. Ethan was horrified to hear the news, feeling overcome with guilt that he had left her there and taken so long to return.

Ethan and Mary rushed to Abigail's room to see her. Abigail lay still on the bed, unable to respond to Ethan's cries to wake her. Ethan knelt beside the bed and held Abigail's hand in his.

Abigail slowly opened her eyes after several minutes. "Ethan," she murmured.

"Abigail," he whispered hoarsely. "I never should have left you. Forgive me, please."

"I am the one who is sorry, Ethan," she responded. "I am dying."

"No you are not, you will be alright. William will be here soon," Ethan replied, his voice full of panic. "You will recover and we will be married on Saturday."

"I wish we could," she said. "It is too late now."

"It is not too late. I will help you however I can. Just

tell me what you need, and I will bring it for you," he said frantically. "Do you want a drink of water? The others say you have had nothing all day."

"I need my mother's rosary," she whispered. "It is in the top drawer."

Ethan leapt from the floor to retrieve the rosary and gave it to Abigail with his hands shaking. "Anything else you need, I am here. Just tell me."

"I must give confession," she said weakly. Tears ran down the sides of her face. "There is a priest who lives near the Valentis."

Ethan turned to hurry from the room until he felt a strong hand on his shoulder. "What does she need, Son?" asked his father's voice.

"She is asking for a priest who lives up the road from the farmhouse," Ethan replied, clutching his stomach in agony.

"I will get him. You stay with her," his father told him. Ethan nodded gratefully and John hurried out of the house to the stable. He climbed on a horse and rode away to find the priest as quickly as possible.

Mrs. Price arranged for Louisa to stay in one of the upstairs rooms while the others were looking in on Abigail. Louisa felt helpless and wished that she could do something to assist the anguished family.

Mary was beside herself with worry. Ethan stayed kneeling by the bed as he talked with Abigail about the estate that he was inheriting. "There is a cheerful cottage that I think you would like to live in," he explained. "And if you do not like the cottage, we can live in the house of course. It has fifty rooms."

Abigail managed a smile. "I love you," she whispered.

Ethan held her close against his chest as tears rolled down his face. "I love you, Abigail. Please—stay with me."

"William is here," Clara announced solemnly from the hallway. William soon came through the doorway of Abigail's room. Ethan moved from Abigail's bedside to make room for him. Clara and Mrs. Price retired to bed so they would not crowd the small room.

"Abigail," William said gently to her. "When did the fever start?"

"Yesterday," she answered wearily.

"I am trying to understand how you became ill when the others in the house have not. Is there anything you might have eaten, or a well you might have drank from, apart from the others ?" he asked urgently.

"I do not think so," she replied. "You need not attend to me, William. There are others who need you more. I am dying."

"I have seen countless cases of this fever, and many patients recover, Abigail," he tried to assure her.

"But—I have seen my mother. She lives in a beautiful place in Heaven. She came to me and told me that everything would be alright."

William felt his heart sink. He tried to swallow the lump in his throat. "Just stay with us, Abigail. You are loved and needed here."

John Smith walked through the door with Father Salvestro just before leaving for the outdoors to be sure he was not in anyone's way. William looked up at the priest in confusion.

"Abigail has asked to give confession," Ethan quietly explained to William.

"We should let her," William answered, gently squeezing Abigail's hand, and moving to make way for the priest.

Mary approached William in the upstairs hallway. "How bad is she? Please, tell me the truth."

William could hardly answer her. When he finally did, his voice was shaking. "You should prepare yourself, Mary."

"Dear God, no!" Mary cried in a whisper as she covered her face with her hands. "Is there anything we can do?"

"We can make her comfortable and try to get her to drink," he replied. "And pray with all our strength that she lives through the night."

Mary nodded and waited in sorrow as Abigail quietly gave her confession to the priest. After several minutes, the priest rose from her bedside and backed away.

"She is asking for you now, Mary," Ethan said.

Mary went to kneel beside Abigail. "I am here. Is there anything I may do to help?"

"Mary," Abigail smiled slightly, but her voice was weak. "I wish you to keep my dearest possession when I am gone—my mother's rosary—if you don't mind."

Mary could not contain the tears that flowed freely as she gazed at the rosary that Abigail held. "It is beautiful," she answered. "I hope that you may keep it for many years to come." It took great effort for Mary to stand up. Her body felt heavier than it ever had with each strenuous step she took away from Abigail's side. Ethan went back to be with Abigail while Mary met William in the hallway.

"She really believes that she is dying!" cried Mary in a whisper. "I cannot live without her."

"I am sorry, Mary," said William sadly. "This is the most terrible visit I have had to make. I came as soon as I was able, but I do not know of anything further I can do for her." His sad eyes looked weary with dark circles underneath them. It was clear that he had not slept in days.

"I will show you to a bedroom where you can rest," Mary said in a low voice. She led him to a nearby guest room.

"Thank you, Mary," he said as he sat on the bed. He was asleep within seconds. Mary left quietly and returned to see Abigail. As she walked into the room, she could see Ethan pleading with the priest.

"Sir—Father, Abigail wishes to be married. Can you marry us now? I will convert. I will do anything I must, just tell me what I have to do to marry her tonight," he said urgently.

Father Salvestro looked downcast at Ethan. "My heart is heavy for having to answer you that I am not permitted to marry you under the circumstances. Conversion is a process that cannot be accomplished in one night."

Ethan dropped to his knees and wept into his hands while Mary and Father Salvestro looked on helplessly. The priest returned to Abigail as he thought about the final words he might say to her. "Abigail, do you wish to be married to this man tonight?" he asked about Ethan.

"I do wish it, Father. If only it were possible," she replied in a whisper. "I can hear him crying."

"Young man?" called the priest. Ethan quickly got to his feet and joined him. The priest continued, "There is a way you may be married tonight if it is what the both of you wish. I cannot marry you into the Church, but I can be a witness. If you declare yourselves now to be man and wife, and live together as married from this day forward, your marriage will be as lawful as the most elaborate ceremony could make it."

"Truly?" Ethan asked hopefully. "Yes, I wish to declare it as you said."

"Abigail, do you declare yourself to be this man's wife?" asked the priest.

"Yes," she answered softly.

"And Young Man, is this the woman you declare to be your wife?"

"She is," Ethan answered.

"Then I am a witness to your declaration and agree that you are lawfully married."

"But Father," said Abigail worriedly. "Will we be married in the eyes of God?"

The priest held back the tears that threatened to release at any moment. "I believe you will be, Child," he answered in a whisper.

Mary observed everything that was said while holding a handkerchief to her tear-stained face. The priest soon left the house and Ethan lay on the bed next to Abigail with his arm carefully draped around her waist. Mary left the room quietly and planned to cry herself to sleep that night, praying to see Abigail recovered the next day.

"Ethan," Abigail said suddenly. "Tell William that I bought poundies from an Irish boy in the street. I have just remembered. Please tell William to be kind to the poor boy. His family has nothing."

Ethan did not understand the importance of the words that she spoke to him, but he assured her that he would relay the message to William. Abigail then closed her eyes. She did not respond to Ethan any longer. Ethan panicked and called in an anguished voice so loud that it struck fear into the hearts of everyone in the house, "William!"

William awoke with a start and rushed to the room where Abigail was limp on the bed. He breathed in relief. "She still lives, but she is unconscious. When Abigail wakes again, give her water, if she will take it."

"I will," Ethan replied breathlessly, trying to recover from his fright. "She said to tell you that she bought poundies from a boy in town, and that you should be kind to him."

"What does that mean?" William asked him.

"I did not understand her either," Ethan answered helplessly.

"Forgive me for interrupting," Bridget spoke timidly from the hallway. "Poundies are potatoes with gravy, Dr. Hamilton."

A look of realization crossed William's face. "She was trying to tell us what made her ill. I think that I know the boy of whom she speaks. I have not seen him the past several days, but I will see to it that his family is notified discreetly."

Ethan nodded and lay down next to Abigail again. William left the room and closed the door behind him. Mary was waiting in the hallway with wide eyes.

"Is she—?"

"She still breathes, Mary, but the fever has not subsided," William explained. "You should try to sleep. Tomorrow may be another long day."

"I will not sleep tonight," she answered. I have just ordered tea."

"I see. I will stay up also, if you wish," offered William. Mary led him to the upstairs sitting room where William stirred the fire. They sat in front of the fireplace and drank tea together, never saying a word of what they were thinking.

CHAPTER 12

Ethan awoke suddenly the next morning. Memories of the night before gradually came to his recollection. He could feel his eyes and face burning from his cries of heartbreak that did not cease until he fell asleep. He quickly reached out his arm to hold Abigail, but could no longer feel her lying next to him. Ethan sat up straight in bed and looked beside him. He could only see the bed sheet and pillow. Abigail was not there.

The door to the en-suite bathroom opened just then and Abigail stepped into the room. "Good morning," she greeted cheerfully.

Ethan stared at her in astonishment while she climbed back into the bed. "How—how are you feeling?" he stammered.

"I feel better than I have in a long time," she answered with a smile. "I had a lovely dream that you and I were married in this very room."

"You are remembering what happened last night," he told her, still amazed that Abigail seemed to be awake and in good spirits.

She clasped her hands together in delight. "Then it

wasn't only a dream! I did enjoy waking up beside you this morning."

Ethan gazed at her lovingly and stroked her hair. "Are you sure you are alright? Is there anything that I can bring for you?"

"You had better not leave me just now," she replied playfully. "I am your wife and I am still waiting for you to kiss me." Abigail smiled as Ethan moved closer to her on the bed and soon held her in a passionate embrace.

In the upstairs sitting room, Mary awoke with a start to sunlight flowing in through the large windows. She was still on the settee next to William where they had both fallen asleep the night before. Mary stood up quickly and William opened his eyes. He looked around the room groggily until he remembered how he had gotten there.

"Should we check on Abigail?" Mary questioned him.

"Let us see if Ethan has left the room," William answered. They quietly walked down the hallway toward the bedroom just in time to see Ethan emerge and close the door behind him. He appeared to be in a blissful daze. One look at Ethan caused William to chuckle. "Abigail is recovered," he whispered to Mary.

"She is? How do you know?" Mary asked bewildered.

Ethan was smiling sheepishly as he approached Mary and William. "She is asking for breakfast," he told them.

"I suggest you hurry," William laughed. "Be sure that she drinks water today." Ethan nodded and headed for the kitchen.

Mary sighed in relief. "Thank goodness she is alright. What a fright she gave us!"

"I am going to return to town now, Mary. I need to

look in at the clinic and attempt to find the boy who might have caused the outbreak. I—I am happy that your friend is recovering. The only patients of mine who never woke again were the ones who reported visits from their departed relatives. When Abigail told me that she saw her mother— I nearly broke down, thinking of what it would do to you."

"I am glad you did not tell me this last night, or I might have fainted. I believe that I will sleep well today knowing my dear friend is alright. When will I see you again?" Mary asked him.

"I am not sure," William answered. "Abigail should be just fine as long as she continues to eat and drink."

Mary nodded. "Thank you for coming here for Abigail. Will you telephone us when the outbreak is over?"

"I will," he promised. "Goodbye, Mary."

Everyone was able to breathe easy when the news of Abigail's recovery spread through the house. Mrs. Price told Clara, who was still lying in bed. Clara reacted gratefully, but it looked as though her mother had more to say. "There is something else, Child," Mrs. Price continued. "It is about your chauffeur. He was bothering the maids last night and I saw to it that he left the estate."

Clara shrugged. "I did not like him much anyway," she stated bluntly.

"I wonder if you would consider Mr. Valenti for the position. He is a good man, Clara—even if he is a Catholic."

Clara looked up in surprise. "I never imagined that you would admit such a thing."

Mrs. Price smiled bashfully. "I may be set in my ways, but on rare occasion it is possible for my mind to change."

"It would be agreeable to me, if Phillip does not mind. Do you really think he would want to chauffeur for me?"

"I think he will do what he must to feed his family. I will speak with him after breakfast," decided Mrs. Price.

Mary went to the gardens behind the house and found John Smith working away as usual. "The gardens are looking lovelier than they ever have. It is a shame there will not be a wedding this weekend," she mentioned.

The pair of shears that John held in his hand dropped to the ground as he looked at Mary in horror. "She is—gone?"

"Oh! I thought that everyone had heard by now that Abigail has recovered. I am sorry to frighten you! I only meant that she and Ethan will not be married in the gardens as they planned. They were married the presence of the priest last night."

John nodded in relief. "Good for them. I sure was worried for that sweet girl."

"Um—Father—," Mary said awkwardly. "Will you be happy living in the manor house with us?"

"I don't know that I could. Too many memories. I have been thinking about Louisa's idea of going West. I always wanted to be a cowboy, you know."

Mary giggled. "I did not know. I do hope you join us for breakfast and tell us about your plans."

John smiled. "If you insist, Miss Mary."

Mary and John arrived at breakfast where Clara, Mrs. Price, and Louisa were already seated. Mary made introductions and Clara was pleased to be hostess to her first guest since she became Mistress of the house. Mary told them the wedding story of Abigail and Ethan from the night before. The ladies felt tears in their eyes as Mary recounted the details.

"It may be the most romantic wedding that I have ever heard of," remarked Clara. "I planned to make Abigail's wedding a grand affair, but the way it happened will surely be more memorable than any other wedding could have been. If only she had not been so ill, poor dear."

"We should send word to the minister that we will not require his services after all," Mary thought aloud. "I nearly forgot to ask—how was your time in New York, Clara?"

"It was marvelous," Clara answered beaming. "I am in love with it already and I intend to go more often. I hope you will accompany me sometime, Mary."

"I do have news of my own to tell you. I now understand why Father did not choose to recognize me in his last wishes. My Aunt Louisa has explained everything and transferred her estate to Ethan and me. It has a lovely manor house with spectacular gardens. I cannot wait to show it to you, Clara."

"Mary, that is excellent news! I have felt guilty ever since Davenport House was settled upon me. I am relieved to know that you will have a grand house of your own," Clara replied.

Louisa smiled shyly. "I am delighted that the manor house will be left in such deserving hands. I believe that my sister would be pleased to know that her children are well set up in life."

John looked intently at Louisa from across the table. "Thank you," he said quietly. Louisa returned his look and smiled.

After breakfast, Mrs. Price went into the kitchen to see

her sister Catherine. "I have something to tell you, Sister," she began. "I have crossed paths with the former cook of this house. She wishes to return. We made an agreement that in exchange for documents in her possession, I would reinstate her as cook for Davenport House."

Catherine's mouth hung open. "Why, I never! How could you agree to such a thing, Dorothy Price? I am your own sister and you would throw me out for a second-rate cook! What does Clara say? I will have a word with her this instant—"

"Catherine, please," interrupted Mrs. Price. "You have not let me finish explaining. Clara and I would like you to move upstairs with us as a member of the family."

Catherine raised her eyebrows as the expression on her red face went from anger to elation. She pulled the apron off over her head and threw it in the air. "Why didn't you say so in the first place?" she laughed. "To think—me—living upstairs!" Mrs. Price chuckled as she left the kitchen, satisfied that all would be well with her sister.

John invited Louisa to see the gardens before she left the house that day. Louisa seemed glad to accompany him. They walked together at a leisurely pace as John offered information on each aspect of the gardens down to the last detail. "You seem happy here, John," Louisa observed. "I am glad that I came to visit, and that you were still working here."

John took a deep breath while he summoned the courage to say what was on his mind. "Louisa, I've been thinking about you going West all by yourself. I think it would be good if you had a man with you. I heard it is no place for a woman by herself."

"I see. Do you—have someone in mind?" she asked shyly.

"Well, I was hoping it would be me," he blurted, looking at the ground. He glanced at Louisa quickly to see her reaction. Her cheeks were turning as pink as the roses behind her.

"You wish to go West with me?" she questioned.

"I will go anywhere with you. I would care for you and protect you…for as long as you would let me," he told her. "It is the least I can do. It is—what I want to do."

At the Valentis' farmhouse, Phillip's sister Serena answered a knock at the door. Fiona was standing there nervously, holding a basket of fresh goods from the kitchen. "Good afternoon," Fiona greeted. "I am the housekeeper at Davenport House and I have brought this basket for Mr. Valenti."

Serena smiled. "How kind. Thank you," she said to Fiona. "I will be sure that he receives it."

"Thank you, Miss," Fiona replied. She managed a smile and turned to walk back to Davenport House.

"Who was that?" asked Phillip when he walked into the kitchen.

"It was the housekeeper from the grand house," answered Serena. "She brought this for you."

"That was kind of her," Phillip remarked, rummaging through the cakes in the basket.

"She is sweet on you," Serena said with a smile.

"Who? Fiona? She is a kind girl. She is only being neighborly."

Serena raised her eyebrow. "I know how a girl looks when she is being neighborly, and how she looks when she is sweet on my own brother. You always did have a way of attracting the girls."

Phillip tried to hide his smile. "Hush now, or I will not share any of these fine cakes with you," he teased.

Mary and John Smith stood in front of the house to say goodbye to Louisa, who was soon on her way to Philadelphia. "Miss Mary?" asked John before Mary went into the house.

Mary giggled. "Why don't we try to address each other as family now. I will even call you Father."

Her father smiled. "Very well…Mary. Have you already told the minister that he should not come on Saturday?"

"I was going to send him a post but I worry that he will not receive it in time," she replied. "I may need to visit him in town to explain."

"Well—the thing is—I expect we may need the minister to come after all," he said nervously.

Mary was bewildered. "For what reason?"

"For a marriage ceremony. Me and Louisa," he replied quietly.

Mary gasped. "Truly?"

Her father nodded. "I hope that my children might be agreeable to it."

Mary stepped toward him and kissed his cheek. "I think I may speak for my brother when I say we only want to see you happy…Father."

Fiona entered Abigail's bedroom with fresh linens. "How are you feeling, Miss Abigail?" she asked.

"I am much better. Thank you for caring for me when I was ill. I heard that you ran to the farmhouse to send Phillip for Dr. Hamilton."

"I did, Miss. I am afraid I did not know how to use the telephone," Fiona confessed.

"I am still grateful to you. I must thank Phillip the next time I see him for going for the doctor."

"Yes, Mr. Valenti was very helpful that night," Fiona recalled. "I went to deliver some cakes from the kitchen to him today, but a lady answered the door."

"It must have been his sister," explained Abigail. "Serena came from Pittsburgh to help Phillip with the children."

"Oh," Fiona replied, trying to hide her relief. "Is there anything else you need from downstairs, Miss Abigail?"

"I am alright for now," Abigail answered. "Thank you, Fiona."

When Fiona returned to the servants' quarters, she found Bridget tidying the lobby. "Did you take the basket to Mr. Valenti?" Bridget asked her.

"I delivered it to his house, but Mr. Valenti was not there. I was unable to thank him in person," Fiona answered, seeming disappointed.

"I am sure we will see him another time," said Bridget. "I am only grateful that he arrived when he did last night!"

Fiona nodded in agreement. Her solemn expression then changed into a smile. "Just one of his arms is nearly as big around as my waist! I wonder if he was ever a boxer. He is built like one."

Bridget giggled. "How would you know what a boxer is like?"

"You are too young to remember, but Father used to fight."

Bridget gasped. "He didn't! Mother would never allow such a thing!"

Fiona laughed. "Mother made him stop. She said she was exhausted of nursing his injuries when she had the children to look after on top of it all. Father may have been a fierce fighter, but he was no match for the guilt that Mother could heap upon him."

The girls laughed heartily to envision it. Then Bridget asked, "Fiona, do you think that Mr. Valenti is handsome?"

Fiona felt her cheeks begin to burn and she covered her face. "Even more so, after he helped us last night," she replied in a whisper.

Bridget smiled. "Perhaps you will marry him and live happily ever after in his beautiful farmhouse."

"You must never suggest such a thing like this to anyone, Bridget," Fiona told her sternly. "Father would disown me in an instant if he thought that I would marry an Italian!"

"Well...would you?" asked Bridget.

"Housekeepers do not marry," Fiona sighed. "But if they did, and if Mr. Valenti were ever to ask me...I think that I would like to very much."

Mary hurried into the library to telephone William. "You will never believe who is to get married on Saturday!" she began.

"It might be painful for me to guess, so you had better just tell me," William replied.

"It is my father, John Smith!" she answered dramatically.

"John?" William asked in disbelief. "To who?"

"It is to my aunt. Oh William, there is much that I have to tell you. You will not believe all that has happened since we last spoke properly."

"I believe you, Mary," he said quietly.

"Is anything the matter? Has the outbreak become worse?"

"No, it appears to be over, thank goodness. You may tell Abigail that I spoke with the family of the boy who was selling food on the street. They said that a lady in town had been generous to their family and they had not needed to sell any more since that day. I believe this is the last we will see of the fever for now," William said, sounding as though he was stifling a yawn. "I hope the clinic stays quiet the remainder of the week so that I can sleep."

"But you will come for the wedding, won't you? It will be held in the gardens at noon," said Mary. "I know you and my father have been good friends."

"It is true. Of course I will be there."

Mary smiled. "I look forward to seeing you Saturday."

"Thank you," he answered. "Goodbye, Mary."

Chapter 13

The day of the wedding arrived and Mary was busy looking through her wardrobe, deciding for the tenth time what she would wear to the ceremony. Abigail entered the room unexpectedly. Mary gasped. "I have not seen you in days!" she exclaimed.

Abigail smiled cheerfully. "I have come to give you something, but you must close your eyes. It is a surprise."

Mary giggled and closed her eyes. Bridget quietly followed Abigail into Mary's room, carrying the surprise over her arms before she laid it out neatly on the bed. "Open your eyes now, Mary," Abigail instructed.

Mary opened her eyes. There on the bed before her was the wedding gown that Ethan had given to Abigail. Mary hugged Abigail tightly. "Are you certain?" she asked.

"I will not be wearing the dress, and it really should have been yours anyway, Mary. You can be married in your mother's wedding gown," she replied kindly. "Do you realize that we are sisters now?"

"It seems too good to be true. I was worried for you when you had the fever," Mary recalled emotionally.

"I am recovered now. You need not worry, Ethan has taken great care of me. He also told me of a cottage on the estate from your aunt. Have you seen it?" asked Abigail.

"It is a charming cottage, Abigail. But if it is not to your liking, there are dozens of rooms to choose from in the house," Mary laughed.

"I feel like a princess on her way to a castle. After your father is married this afternoon, Ethan and I will take the carriage to the manor house. We hope to live there before summer is over," Abigail explained.

"Oh, I see," Mary replied quietly. "I will miss you dearly."

"Won't you be wanting to live there yourself?" Abigail questioned.

Mary sighed. "I am worried that it will be too far from William if I go. Oh Abigail, I am worried that he has changed his mind about me. I cannot leave for Philadelphia now while things between us are uncertain."

"You should talk to him, Mary. Perhaps it is only a misunderstanding," Abigail suggested.

"I am hoping to find out today. Tell me, should I wear the blue dress or the green?" Mary asked.

Abigail smiled. "Oh, do go with the blue. It is darling on you and brings out the blue in your eyes."

"The blue dress it is," said Mary. She turned to Bridget, who had waited patiently in the room for Mary's instruction. "Bridget, I have decided. Let us hurry, for we do not have much time."

The ceremony was about to begin. Several chairs had been set out for the guests, which only consisted of Dr. Hamilton and everyone who lived in the house. Mrs. Price wore a cheerful pastel dress, much to her daughter's delight.

The others hardly recognized Mrs. Price at first, since she was not wearing her usual black frock.

Mary helped attend to Louisa, who wore a simple white afternoon dress for the ceremony. Louisa and John were soon standing in front of the minister amid rows and rows of flowers in full bloom. The others made sure that the seat next to Mary was left vacant for William. Mary smiled at him when he sat next to her. "Good afternoon, Dr. Hamilton," she said, looking into his eyes. She could not understand why he did not seem as happy to see her as she was to see him.

"You are wearing colors again," he remarked. "You look lovely, Mary."

Mary blushed. "Thank you," she whispered. The ceremony began. Mary hoped that William would hold her hand, but instead he sat rigidly in his chair, staring straight ahead. Mary could tell that something was wrong. She did not mean to ignore John and Louisa's special moment, but she did hope that it would soon be over so that she could speak with William.

When the ceremony ended, William abruptly rose from his seat and left to shake hands with the groom. Mary looked helplessly at Abigail, who also observed William's eagerness to leave Mary's side. "You must talk to him, Mary," whispered Abigail. "I thought you were only worrying too much before, but he does appear to be acting strange."

"Now that you have confirmed it, I feel more nervous than I did before! What if he has found someone else and does not want to tell me?" Mary anguished over the thought of it.

"You must hurry, Mary. It appears as though he is leaving," urged Abigail. Mary turned to see William hurrying around the corner of the house to return to the front drive. She rose from her seat and followed him as quickly as she could. His long strides were no match for her short ones confined by the skirt of her dress. She was soon holding her skirt in her hands and running toward him.

"William! Wait, please!" she cried, even though she knew it was unladylike to do so.

William stopped walking so that Mary was able to catch up. He turned around to face her. "Mary," he said gently. "I was just leaving. Thank you for your kind invitation."

"I hoped that you would stay so that I could tell you my news," Mary said breathlessly.

William looked down at the ground. "I have already received a visit from…your fiance," he said in a low voice.

"My what?" Mary asked incredulously. "I cannot imagine who you mean."

William was both perplexed and hopeful at her answer. "Then it isn't true?"

"I have never been engaged," she replied. "Who was this person?"

"I have never seen him before. He came to the clinic to tell me to stop seeing you. He said you were engaged to be married."

Mary huffed angrily. "It must have been that Charles Squire. Even I have never seen him before. The woman who I thought was my mother tried to force me to marry him. It is why I moved into the stable and told you I could not receive you at the house anymore."

"You moved into the stable?" William asked. "Mary, I do not understand what is happening with your house, but

I kept away because I dreaded hearing you speak of marrying another man."

"I had no idea that you'd heard of him," Mary explained. "It is a relief to finally hear the reason. I was afraid it was you who had found someone else."

"No, I could not even think of it. But what is the news you were going to tell me?" William asked.

"There is so much to tell. I have lost Davenport House, but at the same time, I have inherited a manor house near Philadelphia."

"Oh, I see. Then, you will be moving there?"

"I don't want to be away from you," Mary replied seriously. She was not going to wait for William to to kiss her this time. She put her arms around his neck and stood on her tiptoes to reach his face with hers.

Phillip Valenti walked around to the gardens to find the newlyweds. He would be driving them to the train station soon. Ethan approached Phillip gratefully. "I never got a chance to thank you for watching over the house while I was away," Ethan said to him. "And for going for the doctor when my wife was ill."

Phillip smiled and gave Ethan a strong handshake. "It was an honor. I am glad that Abigail has recovered. If you ever need anything, you know where to find me."

Clara was looking at Phillip when he was not watching. She thought about how much she regretted parting with him the way she did. Perhaps it was not so bad that they had a difference of beliefs. Even Mrs. Price seemed to approve of him now. Clara gazed at Phillip thoughtfully, wondering what her life would be like if it was her wedding that was taking place today instead of John and Louisa's.

Abigail went to have some cake where Bridget was serving it in the garden. "Thank you, dear Bridget," Abigail told her.

"Miss Abigail," Bridget said timidly. "I heard you speak to Miss Mary about moving to the other house. I wonder if you might take me with you. I can cook and clean. You will need assistance with all of the babies that you and Mr. Ethan will have. I can help with it all."

"It is kind of you to want to come with me," Abigail replied. "I must ask Clara first so she does not think that I am stealing her staff. I would love to have you, Bridget."

"Thank you, Miss Abigail!" Bridget exclaimed. Fiona soon came to assist Bridget in serving the cake.

"Fiona," Bridget whispered when they were alone. "I have requested for Miss Abigail to take me with her when she moves to the manor house."

"I will miss you dearly," Fiona replied sadly. "But I know how much you care for her."

"Perhaps she will need a new housekeeper as well," Bridget suggested.

Fiona smiled. "I could not let Miss Clara down when so many other changes are taking place," she said thoughtfully. Fiona then glanced toward Phillip who was speaking with the other men. "Besides, I believe that I would like to stay at Davenport House for at least a little while longer."

Mary and William were still standing together near the far side of the house where no one else could see them. It felt to them as if time had ceased to exist and they were the only two people in the world. Mary did not remember that just minutes ago, she had been attending a wedding in the gardens. She was now closing her eyes, basking in the waves of exhilaration that washed over her when she felt William kissing her back. She hoped that the feeling would never end, but she opened her eyes again when she could feel William gradually pulling away. "Mary," he whispered. "Do you realize that we have been kissing all this while?"

"Yes," she whispered back. "Isn't it wonderful?"

"It is wonderful indeed, but I believe that your father will be leaving for the train station at any moment now."

"Yes, I expect he will," Mary replied distractedly as she continued to hold onto William and kiss his face.

William laughed softly against her cheek. "But Mary… there is something that I would like to ask your father before he leaves."

Mary sighed dreamily. "Very well," she said, reluctant to pull away and return her arms to her sides. "But I do hope you will come back to me after you have done so."

William smiled. "Of course I will come back. There is something that I would like to ask you as well—something that I have wanted to ask you for a long time."

…excerpt from Book 4…

DAVENPORT HOUSE

Heiress Interrupted

MARIE SILK

"You should sit down for this, Nellie," Mr. Whitmore suggested. Nellie seated herself next to her mother, who appeared unusually pale and wore a shawl around her shoulders.

"Are you feeling ill, Mother?" Nellie asked in concern.

"I am with child, Nellie," Mrs. Whitmore answered softly.

Nellie raised her eyebrows in surprise. "Oh, Mother, how wonderful! I adore babies."

"This changes things for you, Nellie," her father continued in a business-like manner. "It is a family tradition for the eldest male to inherit entirely. Your mother and I have chosen to keep this tradition, if we indeed have a son."

"Do you mean to say that I will inherit nothing if the baby is a boy?" questioned Nellie.

"You understand correctly. However, if we are to have another daughter, the fortune will be divided between the two of you equally," her father answered.

Nellie stared in bewilderment. She had never considered that she could lose her inheritance. It was a certainty that she had taken for granted her whole life. "But, how will I live?" Nellie asked.

"This is why we we wish to send you to London," replied her father. "We hope to see you make a favorable match for which we will even supply a dowry. It is not the way that I would prefer it, but you insist that you are unable to find a husband in America. Your Aunt Lucinda has already lined up potential suitors who are sure to meet with my approval."

"You never approve of *my* choices," Nellie pouted.

Mr. Whitmore rolled his eyes. "If this is about that stable boy again, I will not hear another word of it. I do not even want you associating with the Davenports. That family is in the midst of a loathsome scandal."

"But Mary is my dearest friend," Nellie protested. "She had nothing to do with the dreadful actions of her family."

"That family cost us five hundred dollars this year. My decision is final. Do not be so gloomy, Nellie. You will soon be sailing on the Lusitania and meeting new friends of desirable standing."

About the Author

Marie Silk has enjoyed writing stories and plays since her childhood years. She lives with her family in the United States and frequently travels the globe to learn more about the world and the people in it. Marie is inspired by history and the feats of humanity from ancient civilization to present day. The *Davenport House* historical fiction saga is her first published series.

Emails may be sent to mariesilkpublishing@gmail.com.

Made in the USA
Middletown, DE
18 December 2020